First Publication: 2006 by Samhain Publishing
under the author name Anne Whitfield.
Second Publication: February 2014 by AnneMarie
Brear at Smashwords.
Cover design by Image: AnneMarie Brear

Kitty McKenzie

Published novels:
<u>Historical</u>

Kitty McKenzie
Kitty McKenzie's Land
Southern Sons
To Gain What's Lost
Isabelle's Choice
Nicola's Virtue
Aurora's Pride
Grace's Courage
Eden's Conflict
Catrina's Return
Where Rainbow's End
Broken Hero
The Promise of Tomorrow
The Slum Angel

<u>Marsh Saga Series</u>

Millie
Christmas at the Chateau
Prue

<u>Contemporary</u>

Long Distance Love
Hooked on You
Where Dragonflies Hover (Dual Timeline)

<u>Short Stories</u>

A New Dawn
Art of Desire
What He Taught Her

MS.

AnneMarie Brear

Kitty McKenzie

AnneMarie Brear

The desire of the moth for the star, Of the night for
the morrow,
The devotion to something afar, From the sphere
of our sorrow.
-Shelley.

Chapter One

York, England, November 1864

From an upstairs window, Katherine McKenzie looked out over York's rooftops into the distance. The pale grey clouds parted, allowing weak sunshine to filter through the bare trees and banish the gloom. Below, two weighty men filled the back of a wagon with the furniture from the house. Her gaze shifted to linger on the sorry cluster of her brothers and sisters. Ranging in age from sixteen to two years old, they stood as one on the lush lawn with their small carryalls placed neatly in front of them. Their pale faces peeking out from beneath hats showed little emotion while stern-looking men came and went from their once warm and happy home. Of course, there was no evidence of that now.

Kitty leaned her forehead against the cool glass and fought the tears that gathered as she stared sightlessly down at her remaining family. All morning, the children had watched and listened as strangers invaded each room, taking notes and sizing up all the possessions once important to the family. They understood little of what was happening, but she had told them to wait outside while she and Rory sorted everything out. So, her brothers and sisters, shocked and confused, did as she instructed, not daring to talk about what they saw. Talking would come later.

Inhaling deeply to calm herself, Kitty turned away from the window. Downstairs a variety of men roamed about, murmuring in hushed voices, making notes on what was left to take and how much money each item would bring.

Vultures, that's what Rory called them, but Kitty knew it was all about the cycle of life. She had learned a lot about life in the last few weeks. None of it very encouraging, but nevertheless, it had to be endured.

She sighed, rubbing the back of her neck, stiff with strain. The enormity of what faced her left her cold. Responsibilities had never been hers. There had always been others to care for her comfort. Could she do it? Could she steer the children through this difficult time? As her parents' coffins were lowered into the ground, she promised them she'd keep the family together at all costs. She'd do whatever it took to keep her remaining family safe. As the eldest it was her duty to look after them, but secretly she wondered who would look after her.

Hearing shouts coming from below, she left her parents' empty bedroom and hurried across the landing and down the main red- carpeted staircase.

In the hall, a small gathering watched as two so-called gentlemen wrangled over a large Chinese-painted vase on which each held a firm grip. Making her way to them, Kitty did her best to be polite, even though her anger simmered like a kettle on the stovetop. 'Gentlemen, please. What is the problem?'

A large bearded man turned his florid face to Kitty. His knuckles turned white as his grip tightened on the vase. 'Miss McKenzie, this man is insistent it belongs to him when in actual fact it is reserved for my services rendered.'

The man's breath reeked of alcohol and the fumes washed over her in sickly waves.

'That is a downright lie!' The other man's beady eyes glared at his opponent. 'It says here on my itinerary this particular vase is awarded to my company.'

Kitty ached to be released from this nightmare. Today marked the end of her family's lives as they knew it, and not one of these vultures cared enough to be the least sympathetic. Taking a step closer to the two warring men, Kitty smiled with false sweetness. 'I may be of assistance then.' Without hesitation, she took the vase out of their hands and dropped it onto the hall's marble floor. The shattering porcelain silenced everyone's chatter and the two men gasped in unison.

'There now, gentlemen, no more need to argue over it.' With the last of her dignity and her head held high, she strode down the hall and into the kitchen.

A warmer atmosphere prevailed in the kitchen, as no debt collectors lingered here. A small fire burned in the range and Mrs Flowers, the cook, brewed a pot of tea. Unpaid for many weeks, the kind woman had stayed until the end to help Kitty and the children through this difficult time.

Sitting on an overlooked stool, Kitty smiled gratefully as the older woman gave her a cup of tea.

'How's it goin' in there, miss?' The cook nodded in the direction of the front end of the house.

'Dreadful,' Kitty answered with a sigh, pushing back a stray strand of hair from her face.

Mrs Flowers stirred the milk on the stove in readiness to make hot cocoa for the children. ''Tis indeed a sorry time. Thank the Lord your dear mother didn't live to see this day, it would have broken her heart.' A wistful look crossed her face.

Kitty refrained from commenting. She blamed both of her parents for letting their financial affairs fall into such a state. Now she and Rory must mend the damage. She had adored her parents, but their loving and generous natures not only cost them their lives, but their children's future and happiness. Her parent's inability to manage their funds over the years now left tradesmen and merchants braying for their dues. Now, at nearly twenty-one, she was responsible for not only herself, but also for six family members.

The outside door to the kitchen banged back against the wall. Rory marched in, his usually handsome face red with anger and his blue eyes blazing. 'Do you know what that pompous ass, O'Brien, thinks the horses are worth?'

'No, and neither do I care.' Kitty wiped her hand over her eyes. Tiredness stung them. 'It will not make any difference to us as we'll not see a penny.'

'Father spent good money on them,' Rory defended the animals he adored.

Kitty shot up from her seat, knocking the stool over. Thumping her fist on the table, she glared at her brother. 'Well, if Father had not spent good money on them and other non-essential things, we'd not be in the trouble we are.'

Taken aback by her outburst, Rory's temper rapidly dissipated and he hung his head. 'I'm sorry, Kitty. You are right, of course. None of it is ours anymore and so it doesn't matter a jot. I'm just heart sorry to say goodbye to them, that is all.'

'I know.' She nodded, knowing the shock of all that happened in the last few weeks had not yet taken effect. Losing their parents so unexpectedly not only devastated them, but frightened them too. Then, to learn on the day of the funeral that they must relinquish their home and possessions caused even greater upset. They lived in terror for weeks waiting for this day. No friend or distant relative came to pluck them away from this horrid ordeal.

'Here, Master Rory, will you be kind enough to take this cocoa out to the young ones? They'll be ready for it by now,' Mrs Flowers said with motherly attention. 'I've to be gone in a few minutes to catch the coach.'

Rory left, balancing a tray of steaming cups of hot cocoa, and while Mrs Flowers cleaned up, Kitty went back through the hall to have one more look around her home. The vultures had gone at last. Silence descended like a winter's mist.

In her mind's eye, Kitty could still see the crystal chandeliers. She ran her fingers along the expensive timber panelling and silk wallpaper, which decorated each room of the large house. She toured the drawing room, parlour, front sitting room and library. Laughter and music of previous parties rang in her ears. Her mother was renowned for filling the house with exciting and interesting people. Kitty saw it all as it once was, not as it was now, a combination of cold, empty rooms. She turned to go upstairs just as a wagon driver caught her attention from the front door.

'Excuse me, Miss. This fell out of one of the cupboards when we moved it. I thought you'd like to have it.' He held out a framed painting of her parents on their wedding day.

'Thank you.' Kitty smiled at him and, doffing his cap, he went on his way.

Left alone once more, she gazed down at her parents as they innocently stared at her from their picture. Her father, Jonathan McKenzie, tall and proud in his wedding suit stood behind his new bride, who sat straight and dignified on a chair a little to the left of him. Both Jonathan and Eliza McKenzie had found true love and never hesitated to show it to each other or anyone else. For twenty-two years their love and contentment wrapped a web of happiness around not only themselves but also their whole household. The McKenzie family once held an esteemed position in the community with money, handsome looks, good health and a beautiful house full of children.

The only thing lacking was prudence concerning their finances.

Her mother inherited a large sum of money after the death of her grandmother. Jonathan trained as a doctor, but instead of opening a practice for wealthy clients he preferred to attend the unfortunates of York. Soon enough, Mother's money ran out. Consequently, they borrowed heavily with the bank, hoping a rich bachelor uncle of Jonathan's would pass away and leave Father, as his heir, his fortune. As luck would have it though, the rich uncle still lived and enjoyed his fortune, while her parents became mired in debt and then died premature deaths.

Was it merely four short weeks ago that her father, after visiting patients in the slums, had unwittingly brought death home? Kitty shivered at the memory of how fast the Typhoid took him, her mother and little sister, Davina, just four years old.

The day after their funerals, the collectors of debts, both large and small, came to give her their bills. Father's solicitor, Mr Daniels came to her aid and advised her on the best course of action. Unfortunately, the only solution left was to sell everything. Now they weren't only homeless, but also poor, desperately poor.

* * * *

'Well, that's over.' Kitty locked the front door of the house. She slipped the key under the mat for the solicitor to collect and stopped. For the first time in this whole ordeal she felt her resolve shake. Her home was gone, like her parents. Never again would they hear their parents' laughter ring throughout the house. All the memories within it would die and be replaced with the love and dreams of a new family. It didn't seem right. It wasn't right to lose everything! Why did her parents not ever think of the future?

Gathering her courage, Kitty pulled on her gloves and turned to her remaining family. Six anxious faces looked at her, waiting for her to take control of their lives. Rory, at eighteen, tall and fair-haired, held two-year-old Rosie in his arms. Rosie the youngest and still a baby was the least affected by the going-ons of the last three weeks. Martin, at sixteen, tried hard to be grown up like Rory but his chubby childhood face and innocent blue eyes made Kitty think him still a boy. Mary stood close to Martin. She, at fifteen, was tall and slender with long black hair like their mother's. Next came Joe and Clara, ten and eight, two little fun-loving rascals who kept everyone on their toes but were too adorable to be in trouble for long.

'We had best make a start as we have a long walk to Davygate. Mr Daniels was kind enough to find us some rooms to rent. He even paid for the first week himself.' Kitty smiled, trying to lighten the mood.

'Why must we walk, Kitty? Can we not take the carriage or a cab?' Clara asked, forgetting all Kitty explained to her that morning.

'We no longer have a carriage, pet, nor can we afford to hire a hansom cab. We are all strong and can easily walk to Davygate.'

At the end of the drive, they stopped as their neighbour, Mrs Wentworth, came out to say goodbye. Having lived next door to each other for twenty years, the McKenzies' and the Wentworths' were sociable though not close. Kitty knew Mrs Wentworth believed the McKenzies' to be false pretenders to her class and she had been quite satisfied to see their fall from grace.

'So, my dears. It is time for you to leave?' Mrs Wentworth's gaze flittered over them with barely suppressed glee.

'Yes, Mrs Wentworth. Thank you for being a kind and good neighbour. Goodbye.' Kitty inclined her head to the older women and knew her sarcasm was lost on her. Mrs Wentworth would enjoy holding court at her next tea party, declaring the rumours of their desperate situation to be true. Kitty sighed, what did it matter anymore? Rumours couldn't hurt them now, they were beyond such slights for being homeless and friendless was a far worse condition. She prepared to go on her way, leaving the smaller children to wave.

'Wait, Kitty. I have something for you.' Mrs Wentworth fished in the pocket of her skirt, bringing out a guinea. 'To help you on your way, my dears,' she said with a touch of smugness.

Sensing the other woman's self-importance, Kitty's ire rose. 'Thank you, but no thank you, Mrs Wentworth. As yet we are not reduced to charity.'

Turning on her heel, Kitty motioned for the others to follow, leaving an open-mouthed Mrs Wentworth in their wake.

'Why didn't you take it, Kitty?' Rory said, catching up to her. 'Lord knows we are going to need it.'

Kitty hitched her suitcase handle more comfortably into her hand. 'If it had been anyone else, I would have, but not from her. I never did like her, and she never liked us for all of the smiles she gave us across the lawns.'

They fell into step and walked without talking as they traversed the busy streets of York. Kitty's thoughts whirled around her head as she tried to forget the past and concentrate on the future. The rented rooms would only house them for a week or two. In her reticule Kitty held all the money they possessed, which wasn't much. Soon, she would have to break the news that not only Rory, but also Martin and herself would have to find employment if they were going to live somewhere nice. However, for now she would let it be and just guide the family through their first night away from the only home they had known. For a fleeting moment panic gripped her so powerfully she couldn't breathe. Please, God, let me be strong.

Chapter Two

Rory lifted the heavy brass knocker and rapped it three times.

The green painted door opened to reveal a small round woman with a cheery smile. She ushered them into the hallway. 'The McKenzie family? Oh, welcome, my dears, welcome. I'm Mrs Halloway. Mr Daniels told me all about you. Come this way, this way.' She beckoned them up the staircase into their rooms. Mrs Halloway continued to chatter away while she took Kitty on a tour of the house.

When at last their hostess left them, Kitty massaged her temples to relieve a dreadful headache. She glanced at the tired and miserable children. 'All of you find somewhere to sit and have a rest,' Kitty told them. 'Mrs Halloway is going to send up a tray of food and some tea. Then we will unpack.'

'I don't like it here. I want to go home,' Clara declared.

'Well, we cannot, Clara.' Rory grimaced as he glanced around the room. 'So, the quicker you get used to it the better.'

'There is not much room for us all in here, is there?' Martin spoke. 'No, there isn't, but it will have

to do,' Kitty said. 'At least we didn't have to pay for
it.'

'How long are we going to stay here?' asked Rory,
moving aside the window's curtains to view the
backyard below.

Kitty rubbed her hand over her face. She felt she
could sleep for a week. 'We cannot stay here long, we
don't have the money for it. In fact, we do not have
much money at all.' Kitty paused and looked from
Rory to Martin. 'I wasn't going to say this just yet,
and I hate to say it now, but the three of us will have
to find work and soon.'

'Me?' Martin stared at Kitty.

'Yes, pet. I'm sorry, but there is no other way.'
Kitty put her arm around his shoulders.

Straightening, Martin turned to her. Determination
etched his face. 'It doesn't bother me that I must go
out to work. I'd be pleased to do it.' He grinned. 'You
can rely on me.'

Later, as the others slept, Kitty and Rory sat at the
little table and discussed their future.

Rory turned his teacup around and around. 'Have
you heard from any family friends?'

'No.' Kitty shook her head. 'I'm ashamed that my
pride stops me from sending out more letters for help.
We are near destitute, but I cannot bring myself to
write one more begging letter to people who now
shun us.'

'I cannot believe no one will help.'

'Mother's and Father's friends obviously weren't
really friends at all. Now there are no more parties,
summer picnics and grand balls to enjoy, they have
all mysteriously faded away.'

'I never expected to be in this position. I was
meant to go to university next year.'

She patted his hand. 'I know and I'm sorry your dreams are shattered, but then so are mine.'

'Why did this have to happen? It's all their fault. I hate them for doing this to us. Why couldn't they have paid their bills like everyone else?'

Kitty shook her head. 'I don't know, but what is done is done now. We have to think of us, of keeping out of the workhouse.'

His blue eyes pleaded. 'Don't ever let us walk through those doors, Kitty, promise me.'

'I promise.' Although she had promised, words were easy. Being unskilled and never having done manual labour, she wondered just how she could keep her oath. Despair filled her.

'So, how much money do we have?' Worry creased his brow.

Kitty noticed his blond hair needed cutting. She sighed. 'Not a lot. I managed to gather about forty-five pounds.'

'Forty-five pounds.' Rory jerked back in his chair. 'That is not enough.'

'I'm aware of that, Rory, and keep your voice down,' Kitty admonished, gesturing towards the sleeping children. 'That is why you, Martin and I must find gainful employment as quick as possible, starting tomorrow.'

Rory's eyes widened. 'How are we going to find jobs? We know nothing about working.'

'Yes, I know, but we will learn quickly. We have to.'

* * * *

Kitty thought she knew the city of York well, but after spending all day on her feet tramping from one street to another, she realized the city of her birth was very large and complex. Before, driven by carriage, she and her mother frequented the main streets to shop. Now, at close range and on foot, those streets showed her the beginnings of a huge labyrinth of lanes and alleys. Kitty made a mental note that those back streets held many little shops and small factories. It was these she must investigate if she didn't acquire a job in a more suitable establishment.

As Kitty trod wearily down the narrow, cobbled street towards the lodging house, she saw Joe and Clara sitting on the front step playing marbles. On seeing her, they raced each other to meet her. Joe won and turned to make fun of Clara.

Even though tiredness pulled at her muscles, Kitty smiled at them, glad to see them laughing. After so much recent sadness, it was a welcome change.

In the hallway, Kitty pulled off her gloves. 'I think you shouldn't play in the street. You were never allowed to do it at home.'

Joe shrugged. 'There isn't anywhere else to play. This place doesn't have a yard. How long will we stay here? They have no grass anywhere. How can I play ball?'

'I know it's difficult and not what you are used to, but we—' Suddenly, a side door opened. A tall woman, her angular face stern, came out, barring their way. Her dark brown hair was peppered with grey and pulled severely into a bun at the back of her head. She stared at them with dark beady eyes and raised her chin to peer down her long, sharp nose. 'You are to keep the children upstairs in your rooms at all times.'

A rustle of skirts came from behind them and turning, Kitty saw a flushed Mrs Halloway rushing through the open door carrying parcels of shopping. 'Nancy, you are home early,' she gushed at the tall woman.

'Obviously.' The other woman scowled. 'Where have you been? I've been home since midday.'

Mrs Halloway placed her purchases on the hall table and gave a wry smile. 'I've been shopping and visiting friends. Old Mrs Kettle has a bad chest and I thought I would—'

'I have no time to hear chit chat, but I do want to know why there are children in this building.'

'I meant to write you about the McKenzie family, Nancy.' Mrs Halloway wrung her hands. 'Please, don't be angry. How is Aunt? Is she feeling better?'

'Just answer the question.'

'Yes, I know. I know.' Mrs Halloway's teeth pulled at her bottom lip. She glanced at Kitty. 'Miss McKenzie, this is my sister, Miss Stanley. Nancy, this is Miss McKenzie and her brother and sister.'

Nancy Stanley stood erect, her head turned in the direction of her sister, totally ignoring Kitty and the children. She folded her arms across her flat chest. 'You know my policy about children.'

Mrs Halloway shifted anxiously. 'Yes, but Mr Daniels paid for their rooms in advance. I didn't think it would hurt just this once. They are homeless.'

'And you thought you could get away with it because I was away,' her sister accused. 'I'll return the money to Mr Daniels.'

Mrs Halloway blushed. Tears welled in her eyes as she picked up her shopping and left them.

Nancy Stanley glared at Kitty. 'I do not allow children in these premises. They are disruptive and naughty. My other guests do not wish to be troubled by the noise they make.'

'I assure you, Miss Stanley, the children will be well-behaved.'

She sneered into Kitty's face. 'You'll not be here long enough for them to be anything else. Be gone by morning.' She spun on her heel and left them.

Startled by the demand, Kitty couldn't speak. How can this be happening to us?

She and the children let themselves into their rooms a few minutes later. Taking her coat off, she longed to sit down.

'What is the matter?' Mary asked

'Miss Stanley, the owner of this establishment, does not like children.'

'Oh, I met her today. She knocked on the door because Rosie was crying. She had fallen over and banged her head.'

'Is she all right?' Kitty crossed to pick Rosie up from where she played on a rug with her doll.

'She's fine, just a small bump, but Miss Stanley said if she heard her again, she would throw us out.'

Kitty stared at Mary. 'She said that?'

Mary nodded. 'And she said if she had been here last week when Mr Daniels called, then we would never have been let rooms.'

'Never mind. She told me we must leave in the morning.' Kitty sat at the table and let Rosie climb off her knee. Thoughts whirled around in her head. They had to leave here with nowhere to go. Slowly, she pulled off her shoes and rubbed her aching feet.

'Did you have any luck?' Mary poured Kitty a cup of tea from the small tea tray.

'No, nothing. I think I walked every street in York. Some establishments waved bills at me that Mother owed them. I couldn't risk going to any shop that Mother might have frequented.' She sighed and sipped her tea. 'Mmm... This tea is lovely.'

Mary looked sheepish. 'Yes, well... I'm afraid it has been added to our bill. When Mrs Halloway said at breakfast I could order a tray any time during the day, I didn't think she would charge us for it. I'm sorry.'

Kitty grimaced but reached over and patted her hand. 'Don't worry, you weren't to know.'

'I hope Rory and Martin are able to find work today,' Mary murmured.

'So, do I,' agreed Kitty.

* * * *

After breakfast the following morning, a meal Miss Stanley insisted they eat in their rooms, they packed up their belongings and said farewell to Mrs Halloway. Miss Stanley stood on the doorstep scowling as she watched them walk down the street.

When they turned the corner, Kitty paused on hearing her name being called. Mrs Halloway came stumbling towards them carrying a huge wicker hamper. Rory hurried to help her.

Puffing somewhat, Mrs Halloway put her hands on her hips and took a deep breath, smiling all the while. 'I didn't think I'd be able to sneak out with it.' She panted with a grin. 'I best be getting back before she finds out I'm not there, but first...well, let's just say I'm sorry about how she's treated you and if you're ever in need just get a note to me and I'll do my best to help.' She smiled at each one of them. 'Now, there is enough food in there to last you several days if you take it easy.'

'We'll return the hamper basket as soon as we are settled.' Kitty's voice caught with emotion.

'Good Lord, no lass! Nancy will have a fit if she knows what I have done. No, the basket is yours. We have others, not as big as this one, but this was never used anyway because it was so large.' Mrs Halloway smiled again and ruffled young Joe's hair. 'Take care now.'

'I cannot thank you enough, Mrs Halloway. It is too generous.' Kitty impulsively kissed the older woman's cheek.

'Nay, lass, I wish I could've done more. Well, goodbye now.' She scurried back up the street.

'That was very kind,' Rory said, picking up the hamper.

'Yes, yes it was.' Kitty took Rosie's hand and vowed silently to one day pay back the kindness Mrs Halloway showed them, if not to her, then at least to someone else.

They spent most of the morning seeking rooms to rent. Frustratingly, the better abodes were priced out of Kitty's budget. It was disappointing to be shown sets of neat, tidy rooms or little compact homes with equally small yards knowing they were too expensive for them. Rory and Martin had not obtained work the day before, therefore limiting their options.

As the day wore on, the children grew weary. Finding a decent home was not as easy as she first thought. Kitty shook her head at her ignorance. Fear of the unknown continually reared its ugly head, making her doubt her every decision.

What can I do?

The workhouse came to mind only to be shut out immediately. Never would she knock on that door! She vowed by her parent's grave to always keep the family together and the minute they walked through the workhouse door they'd be separated.

Towards the end of the afternoon, the younger ones whined they couldn't walk any further. Kitty stopped and looked around. Caught up in her dismal thoughts she lost track of where they walked.

They stood in a poor, working class area. Cobbled lanes and close alleys ran off one another. Open sewers filled the narrow streets with filth. Soot-covered buildings, mainly tenement housing, rose up three and four stories, blotting out the weak sun trying to filter down to warm the people swarming the city streets. The smell of rotting vegetable peels, smoke from the numerous chimneys, dampness and refuse filled their nostrils.

Clara held her nose. 'I cannot breathe, Kitty. The stink makes my eyes water.'

'I know, my pet, but we must endure it for a little while.' She smiled her encouragement. They were used to the sweet-smelling gardens of their old home and the fresh air from the countryside that came right up to their long garden at the back of the house.

'What are we to do, Kitty?' asked Rory. 'The weight of this hamper grows heavier with every step.'

'I think we should find somewhere to sleep tonight and then try again in the morning.' She wiped her hair out of her eyes. 'Maybe there's a boarding house close by. Shall we retrace our steps back to the last corner?' She gazed around at the old buildings that appeared certain to topple over any minute. They trudged back the way they came, until, with a cry, Clara stumbled over and fell to the ground.

'Dearest, are you all right?' Kitty crouched to help her. 'My feet hurt.' She wailed. 'My boots are rubbing.' 'There, there. Hush now and let me have a look.'

Taking off Clara's boot, Kitty blanched at the red blisters and angry sores covering the poor girl's foot. It was a wonder she managed to walk at all, obviously Clara wouldn't be able to take another step this day. Kitty glanced up at Rory. 'Run to the corner and ask someone where we can get a bed for the night.'

The landlord of a decaying inn Rory found around the corner, scratched his armpit and leered at Kitty. He sported a large beard and when he opened his mouth it revealed rotted black teeth. 'So, you'll be needin' some rooms for all this lot?' He glared at each of the children.

'Yes.'

'We're not used ter 'avin' many visitors. You'll just 'ave ter tekk what you git.' He rubbed his chin while his gaze roamed appreciatively over her.

'We don't have much money.' Kitty nibbled the inside of her lip, aware that every man in the inn stared at her. She hated their attention. Of course, she knew she held some claim to good looks and wasn't considered plain, but beyond that, she didn't really care if men found her attractive.

The innkeeper grinned and leaned closer. 'Well, lass, with your copper hair and good looks you could earn more money without a problem.'

Insulted, she straightened, wishing she possessed more height than five foot so that she could peer down her nose at the man. His leering as though she was a piece of meat for his choosing made her temper boil. Scanning the room, she noticed grime thick on every surface. Sawdust, riddled with little black insects that came out to crawl over their boots, covered the floor. Out of the corner of her eye, Kitty saw Mary swipe at something creeping up her skirts.

No. She wouldn't do it. She wouldn't make them stay here just to save a few shillings. The way the landlord looked at her she knew, with a woman's born instinct, he would be trouble. The very thought of what state the rooms above would be in made her shudder. Giving Rory a nod, which he understood instantly, she ushered the children out of the small and stuffy taproom and into the street.

'Thank God, you didn't make us stay there.' Rory expelled on a pent- up breath.

Angry at the powers that be and her feeling of uselessness, Kitty turned on him. 'Well, unless we find work and a decent place to live, then it is men like him whom we will have to put up with!'

A passing hackney coach that Kitty promptly hailed to a stop saved Rory from any more of her outburst.

As they all squashed into it, Kitty asked the driver to take them to a reputable hotel. Misery replaced her anger. She turned her head from the others to blink away her tears.

Chapter Three

Kitty reclined back in the bathtub and let the soothing hot water dull her senses. A fire glowed red in the grate, making the room warm. Next door, the three boys were no doubt enjoying the same luxury. It was indeed a waste of good money. However, after all they'd endured since their parents' death, losing their home, the performance in that horrible old inn, plus the agony poor Clara suffered from her feet, Kitty believed they deserved a little pampering. It would have to be a night to last a lifetime.

She shook her head. Of course, after tonight she would have to stop giving in to temptation of getting whatever they wanted, for soon there would be nothing left to pay for it.

A crushing despair swept over her. Never in her wildest imagination had she thought she would end up like this. Her future had been planned for some time, well at least a year or so. She even talked her parents around to her way of thinking. She was to have left at the end of May to go abroad to France and then on to Italy with an elderly friend of her mother's for the summer. On returning to England, she meant to stay with friends in London and maybe apply to become a nurse and take her new skills overseas, like Florence Nightingale, or travel in the footsteps of the intrepid Dr Livingstone. Eventually, she wanted to compile a book about her experiences.

Now, all that was gone. Instead, she had become a member of the working class and surrogate parent for her brothers and sisters. Tears welled in her eyes, but she fought them back. She couldn't weaken now, not when everyone depended on her so much. She must focus on what was important; acquiring a home. Later, when they were settled and happy, she would think about a way of making her dream of traveling come true.

* * * *

As predicted, the hotel bill drained a substantial sum from her money. Kitty shuddered to think of what their situation would be at the end of the day. They made their way through the busy city streets inquiring about places to rent and jobs for Rory and Martin. Just before midday, it rained and within minutes they were wet and despondent. Clara's feet, although heavily bandaged prior to leaving the hotel, bled again. She whimpered with pain.

Plodding down a drenched, slippery lane leading to the River Ouse, Kitty did her best to carry the hamper and her own case, while Rory lifted Clara onto his back and Martin carried Rosie. The rain increased with loud claps of thunder. Lightning streaked the sky and they quickly ran into a sheltered doorway of an old disused warehouse.

'What are we going to do, Kitty?' Rory demanded. 'We cannot keep going on like this.'

Kitty sighed and pushed her wet hair back behind her ears. She had long ago taken off her bedraggled and ruined hat. 'I don't know what to do. We have been in every agent's office in York, I'm sure. None of them have anything we can afford. Maybe it is time we looked for something in the poorer areas.'

'But those places are disgusting.' Rory shifted Clara more comfortably on his back.

Annoyed and tired, Kitty's hunched her shoulders against the cold. 'It's time you understood we're in no position to criticize. Until we have some earnings, we'll just have to put up with whatever we find.'

'I'm not living in some flea infested rat hole.' Rory's face grew red in his frustration as another clap of thunder roared above them.

'Well, you can stay here and live in this doorway for all I care,' Kitty snapped, as rain pelted in at an angle, soaking them. 'Let us go,' she commanded the others.

They walked two more streets before another loud thunderclap and a flash of lightning made them shelter in a doorway of an ancient building.

A woman sharing the cover eyed them suspiciously. She wore plain, patched clothes. Her mousy, brown hair hung lank around her shoulders and her light blue eyes stared at them from a cold, pinched face. 'You lost or summat?'

Looking over Martin's shoulder at her, Kitty smiled. 'Yes, something like that. Actually we are searching for a place to stay.'

The woman peered through her wet hair that dripped onto her face. 'Somewhere ter stay 'round 'ere? Nay, there's nowt for your kind 'round 'ere.'

'We need lodgings, but we don't have much money.'

The woman sniffed, passing a hand across her eyes to clear her vision. 'Have you realized where you are?'

'Yes, but we're desperate.'

The impoverished woman studied her for a moment. Apparently satisfied that Kitty seemed genuine, she indicated down the street. 'There's a cellar goin' beggin' where I live, if you're interested.' She gave Kitty a nod as though to say she was doing her a favour.

'Is it close by?' Kitty ignored Rory's sound of disgust.

'Aye. Follow me, though somebody could've tekken it be now. There's allus a body wantin' a place ter kip.' She moved off into the rain, not waiting for them to gather all their belongings.

Hurrying to catch up, for the woman was a fast walker, Kitty urged the others to keep pace as they made their way into the world of alleys, lanes and back streets.

Tenement buildings of all shapes and ages towered above their heads. The rain sent most people indoors, but a few lingered in their doorways watching the wretched group as they lumbered by. Kitty was aware of their looks and whispers. Women with cold, speculative eyes and children in bare feet and snotty noses jostled one another for position to stare at the newcomers. Here, in the bowels of the city, people lived and breathed poverty. Despair, depression, hunger and the threat of sickness and disease faced them every moment of their lives.

Kitty lost all sense of direction. She presumed they were in the Walmgate slum area. Other than that, she had no idea and, for the moment, didn't care.

The woman didn't speak as they walked and when she suddenly stopped in front of a large, very run-down building, Kitty and the children collectively sighed a breath of relief. They were all tired, sodden and hungry, and longed for just a few minutes' rest out of the heavy rain.

'In there is where I live, first door on't left.' She pointed through the open doorway into the dark interior. 'Just inside the doorway 'ere, there's a set of steps leadin' down t'cellar.'

'Is there someone we should see about it?' Kitty asked tentatively. Sewer filth ran over her boots. Rubbish lined the small alley. She wasn't sure whether she could stand the thought of going inside the building.

They could hear yelling and cursing coming from the rooms above them and somewhere beyond, a baby cried.

The woman began to laugh, a surprisingly cheery laugh. 'Good God, you've got a lot to learn, not that I reckon you'll be 'ere that long.' She stopped laughing as quickly as she started and, with a sniff, led them into the building. Turning swiftly, she descended a set of unbelievably steep stone steps that nearly had them all on their backsides. At the bottom, a broken door leaned into the dim interior beyond.

Tumbling in after each other, the children stopped short, staring in horror at the dark, damp and utterly disgusting dungeon surrounding them. Clara cried again with Rosie joining in from sheer fright.

Rory cleared his throat, but before he had chance to speak, Kitty stepped forward. 'What rent would we have to pay for this?'

'A few bob normally, but we've all stopped payin' until the toff who owns this place fixes it up. His rent man stopped comin' 'ere months ago. We refused t'pay good brass for summat that's about t'fall down around our ears. 'She folded her arms across her chest. An angry flush coloured her cheeks. 'Rent man fears for his life along this alley. He's hated summat fierce.'

Kitty frowned. 'Then no one will mind us staying here?'

'Nope.' The woman turned towards the door. 'Unless you cause trouble. In this buildin' we like t'keep our heads down. You see there's a lot of folk who'll not be happy if the polis started pokin' their noses about. Understand?'

'Yes, yes, of course,' Kitty assured her. 'You won't get any trouble from us.'

'That's right, you won't,' Rory butted in, 'because we're not staying here.'

'We will for the time being, Rory,' Kitty silenced him. 'Simply because there is nowhere else.'

'Well, please yourself.' The woman turned for the door. 'But if you want 'owt, I'm just above your head.'

'Wait! What is your name?'

Glancing over her shoulder, the woman gave her a strange look. 'No one goes much on names 'ere. There's no social club t'join, you know.'

'No, I realize that, but still it would be nice if we could be friends?' She smiled. 'My name is Kitty, Kitty McKenzie. These are my brothers and sisters, Rory, Martin, Mary, Joe, Clara and little Rosie.'

'Aye, well, me name's Connie, Connie Spencer.' With that, she marched up the steps and out of sight.

Kitty turned back to her family and the awful realization of what they stood in. The walls ran slimy with mould. Tiny rivulets of water seeped from the cracks in the bricks. Mildew and stains covered the ceiling and bled down from the floors above. She shuddered, trying not to guess what they might be. Years of dirt, grime and in places, filthy sawdust, swathed the floor. A revolting stench came from somewhere. Kitty hoped to God there wasn't anything dead in here.

Opposite the door was a small fireplace with what looked like some kind of cooking plate across the top of it. A shelf above served as a mantelpiece. Situated at street level, above their heads, their lone window measured roughly two feet wide and three feet long. Thick dust and cobwebs blocked out most of the grey light. The wall to the left of the steps was actually, on closer inspection, made out of very thin wooden boards. Kitty gave it a solid push and it fell away quite easily, exposing another part of the cellar nearly twice as large as the main area.

'Someone must have boarded the room up to help with the heating,' she said.

'We cannot possibly stay here, Kitty! Pigs would live in better conditions I'm sure,' Rory protested.

'I'm sorry, but as I see it we have no choice. It is either here or back out in the rain.'

'We could stay in a hotel tonight and look again tomorrow. We still have some money left,' he pleaded.

'No. On impulse I let us stay at that hotel last night and look how much it cost us. We must use our remaining money wisely or we will be in the workhouse before you know it, and I'll not let that happen.' She stood with her hands on her hips. 'We have to make the most of what we have, which is this cellar for the time being.'

'You expect us to sleep on this filth!' he exploded.

'We are going to clean the place. Just because circumstances have forced us to live here, it doesn't mean we have to live like others do in this area.'

'But we have nothing to clean with,' Mary said.

Kitty grinned at her. Mary was always sensible. 'That will soon change. We'll go to the shops and buy what we need.'

'Oh, that is just marvellous.' Rory's voice rose in anger. 'You're willing to spend money on cleaning materials but not on us having somewhere decent to sleep?'

'Enough Rory!' Kitty rounded on him. 'I have had enough of your whining.' Taking a deep breath to calm herself, she turned to Martin and Joe. 'Now, will you two help me?'

Martin and Joe nodded, their faces pale and lips blue with cold. 'Good. Right, first I want you both to break up all the wooden boards

over there. It will be our first fire.' Kitty peered at the fireplace. Ashes clogged it, but using a piece of wood, she soon cleared it out into a dusty pile on the floor.

Straightening, she went over to their cases and pulled out her small reticule. 'Mary, you stay here and mind everything, while Rory and I go to the shops.' She realized, with a bit of a shock, that she was going to enjoy the challenge of turning this squalid cellar back into some semblance of living quarters. Never before had she been set a task that required so much of a successful outcome. She was determined to do it. They all depended on her sensible judgment. Their well-being firmly rested on her shoulders.

'I'm not coming with you,' Rory cut into her thoughts. 'Fine. Stay here and help clean.'

'I'm not staying here either. If you want to play housemaid, then you can do it on your own.'

For a second Kitty wasn't sure she understood him. 'Rory—'

'I mean it.'

With a shiver of dismay, it dawned on her. 'You're going to leave?'

Rory averted his gaze and retrieved his own case from amongst the others. 'I'm sorry, Kitty, but I cannot stomach staying here another minute.'

She blinked rapidly to throw off her shock. The need to cry swamped her. 'It's still raining. You can't go back out in that and where will you go?'

'I might try some of my friends. The Preston family live along Bootham and they came to Mother and Father's funeral. Maybe, they'll allow me to stay for a night or two until I sort something out.'

'They weren't so eager to help when I sent them a letter before,' she challenged. 'They had all the excuses in the world then.'

'I can try.'

Kitty's heart turned. Panic clawed at her. 'We made a promise at the grave site to always be together. We were supposed to be each other's support through all this.' She couldn't believe he was walking out on her, on them all.

Rory hung his head and Kitty clenched her teeth. He cannot even look at me. She took a deep breath. She didn't want to say something she would later regret.

After a few seconds Rory looked up, then shifted his case in his hands. 'I have to go. I'm sorry, Kitty.' He was close to tears and his chin quivered. 'I cannot stay here in this prison cell.'

'This is only temporary. Please, don't leave.' 'I have to.'

She swallowed her tears. 'V-very well, here.' From her reticule she gave him some of her sorely needed money. 'Here is five pounds. It's all I can spare.' She turned away, going over to where the others stood in amazement at what was happening to their family.

Picking up the broken boards, Kitty cracked them into smaller pieces for kindling. She made enough noise to drown out the quiet weeping as each in turn said goodbye to their eldest brother. How can he do this to us? A sharp pain of betrayal twisted her stomach into knots.

When Rory had been gone for more than five minutes, Kitty discarded the wood and picked up her reticule again. 'I'm going to the shops to buy a few things. Mary, help the children out of their wet clothes. We should have done that first. I wasn't thinking.' Kitty paused to peer at them. They seemed to be all right. However, in the future she must be more careful. She had to be mother, housemaid and every other role to them from now on.

'Martin, Joe, while I'm gone, you two scout about for newspaper to light the fire. Maybe you could ask Mrs Spencer for some matches. I'll get more, but you might be able to find something and start the fire while I'm out. Just be careful and don't go too far. Stay in and about the building.'

Kitty left them and walked up the steps. At the top, she stopped to button her coat and straightened her sad-looking black hat. It no longer rained, but the sky still glowered black and ominous. Behind her, near the stairs leading up to the next floor, a door opened.

Kitty smiled as Connie came out carrying a net shopping bag. 'You are going to the shops as well?'

'Er…aye,' Connie muttered, walking past.

'I was wondering whether we could borrow some matches for the fire and some paper if you have any?'

Nodding, Connie re-entered her own home and within a few moments returned with matches and paper. Kitty called to Martin, who took them gratefully.

Turning back to Connie, Kitty smiled. 'May I walk with you? I don't know my way around this area.'

Connie shrugged. 'Aye, if you want.'

Setting off at a fast pace, Connie didn't speak. Not that Kitty minded, she was far too busy taking notice of what lanes and alleys Connie used. Before long, they were mingling with the scurrying crowd who took advantage of the break in the weather before darkness ascended.

Reaching the market, Connie paused. 'I suppose you'll be needin' a few things then?'

Kitty chuckled. 'Yes, we do.'

'Boyle's Warehouse, just off Goodramgate, they'll have what you want.'

She nodded, but hesitated. 'Could…I mean…would you be able to come with me, if it is not too much trouble for you?'

'I have me own shoppin' ter do.' Connie sniffed.

'Yes, of course you do. I'm sorry.' Kitty blushed and glanced at the sky. It would be dark soon. Saying goodbye to Connie, she lifted her skirts and darted away.

An hour later, Kitty weaved through the crowds in the market. She spent far too much time and money at the warehouse, and now worried about how the children were coping. Dodging a fruit cart being wheeled by an old man, she heard raised voices and paused. A fishmonger haggled with Connie over his prices and a small gathering stopped to watch.

Hanging back, Kitty observed Connie arguing her case. The end result being the fishmonger gave Connie more fish for her money. After it was all over and the throng dispersed, Kitty walked near to where Connie stood counting her money. Not wanting to be rebuffed by her again, Kitty pretended to be interested in buying some vegetables from a stall.

'Don't buy from 'er,' came the whisper in Kitty's ear. Glancing up, she locked gazes with Connie.

'No?'

Connie shook her head and then nodded in the direction of another vegetable stall at the end of the row. As they walked around the market, Kitty kept asking questions and eventually, Connie become a little more at ease. She gave Kitty her knowledge of the market and shopping in general. She told her who supplied the finest produce for the best price and where to buy cheap, but still good, clothing material.

Strolling back through the darkening streets, Kitty told Connie of her circumstances and how Rory's leaving hurt more than she could acknowledge openly to the others. 'He'll come back, of course.' She tutted. 'I doubt he'll stay away for more than one night.'

'He should never have left you.'

'It's hard for him, Mrs Spencer. I cannot blame him or be too harsh on him. He's just as frightened as I am.'

Turning into the lane of their tenement building, they heard cursing. The driver of a delivery wagon struggled to keep the alley children off his goods.

'Oh my. I forgot about the delivery man.' Kitty gathered her skirts up and broke into a run.

'About bloody time,' the driver shouted. 'I was ready to take it all back.' He climbed down from his seat and began unloading her purchases.

Kitty called for the boys before she and Connie helped the driver.

Darkness shadowed the slums by the time everything was off the wagon and piled in the cellar. Iron beds with thin lumpy mattresses, plus pillows, sheets and blankets stacked on top of them were in one corner, while a small, square table, cheaply made, and four chairs packed another corner. Near the fire, which had not been lit despite all of Martin's attempts, stood a pail, a broom and a scrubbing brush, a kettle, a lantern with oil, a box of tallow candles, not wax ones, and lastly a box of economical, incomplete, and terribly ugly by Kitty's standards set of crockery and cutlery.

Earlier at the market, Kitty had bought a bundle of rags as well as soap, tea, sugar, bread, cheese, ham and apples to add to the vastly depleting hamper Mrs Halloway gave them. Finally, she obtained an extra stack of old newspapers to light the fire with.

'My God, you sure know how t'spend up,' Connie commented, as they stood in the midst of it all.

Kitty took off her coat, hat and gloves. 'It'll do to start with.' She grinned, seeing the older woman eye the mess.

'I'll give you a hand, at least for a while, until me husband comes home.'

'Thank you, Mrs Spencer, that is most kind.' Kitty shook her head in wonder at the other woman's complexities.

'Aye well, you know what they say, many hands mean light work.'

With Connie on the broom, and Kitty following her scrubbing like someone demented, they made headway with the cellar's dirt. Clara and Joe, armed with rags tied at the end of pieces of wood, attacked the numerous cobwebs hanging in great necklaces from the ceiling. Martin fetched water from the tap at the end of the lane. It was a hard job lugging the full pail back up to the tenements, but it was the only tap where the water was clean and not turned off. Apparently, so Connie told them, the other tap water at the back of the buildings made people sick.

When Kitty's arm ached from scrubbing, Mary told her to rest and took over. As none of them had worked at domestic duties before, they found it tough going and soon tired. Kitty cleaned out the fireplace with a damp rag and re-laid it with a mountain of paper and pieces of thin broken board. Soon, the fire roared. Flames went so high up the chimney they ignited all the built-up soot.

Tenants living on the higher floors found to their surprise smoke billowing in through cracks in their walls. They panicked, thinking the building was on fire and they would all burn to death.

Connie raked out Kitty's great fire and settled it down to a more acceptable blaze, then went up to the landing to calm everyone.

Kitty dusted her hands together. 'I suppose that's one way of introducing ourselves.'

The warmth of the fire, which burned well due to the chimney being cleared of blockage, put her and the children in better spirits.

Martin grabbed a wet rag. 'Hold my legs, Kitty. I'll clean the window up there.'

'Be careful,' Kitty warned as he placed a chair onto a box and climbed up on it.

Mary lit two candles and put one on each end of the mantelpiece. She took the crockery and cutlery out of the box, setting them neatly on the table along with the food Kitty bought and whatever was left in the hamper.

'I'm hungry.' Joe rubbed his stomach.

'We'll eat in a minute, Joe.' Mary slapped his hand as he reached for a piece of cheese.

They all jumped with fright when a loud voice boomed out a welcome from upstairs. Spinning around, they faced a giant of a man standing at the top of their steps. He must have stood six foot four and weighed twenty stone. His shoulders were big and powerful. He owned a great head of ash blonde hair and bushy eyebrows to match.

'So, a man comes 'ome from a hard day's graft an' all he finds is an empty fireside an' table!' he bellowed. He stared at them for a moment before his expression changed into a large grin and his golden brown eyes softened.

'Nay, I'm that sorry, love.' Connie darted to pick up her shopping she had put down nearly two hours ago. 'Time got away from us.'

'We've new neighbours then?' He grinned.

'Max, these are the McKenzies.' Connie introduced him to each one in turn. 'This is me husband, Max Spencer.'

Kitty noticed how Connie transformed in her husband's presence. Gone was the sour expression and wishy-washy flat blue of her eyes. Instead, they turned into sparkling specks of light. Bright spots of colour appeared on her cheeks.

'We are very pleased to meet you, Mr Spencer,' Kitty said, shaking his hand.

'Nay, lass, I'm just Max. Mr Spencer is me father.' At that he roared with infectious laughter, making them giggle.

Connie took his arm. 'Come on then, let's go an' have some tea.' 'Why don't you share ours?' Kitty offered. 'There is plenty.'

'Why that's a grand offer, lass, but I see you've got enough ter do without seein' t'us as well.' Max's eyes twinkled. 'Perhaps we'll do it another time, hey?'

'Yes, that would be lovely.' She smiled back. 'Good night.'

After the Spencers left, Kitty and Mary placed the three iron beds at the end of the cellar and made them up with the lumpy mattresses, patched sheets, hard pillows and thin blankets.

Kitty and the children sat at the table. Having only four chairs meant Martin and Joe sat on upturned boxes. They ate their simple meal of bread, cheese, ham and fruit with relish. Kitty forgot to buy milk and for the first time ever in their lives the children drank their tea without it.

After such an exhaustive day, the younger children climbed into bed with barely a complaint and cuddled up together to keep warm.

'I wish Rory was here,' Martin murmured, staring into his cup of black tea.

The busy evening caused them to force Rory's departure to the backs of their minds, but now in the settled quiet, their thoughts returned to him.

'It was his choice to go,' stated Kitty, hurt by what she regarded as his cowardice. 'Though, I believe he will return soon.'

Mary glanced about her, and although the cellar was an improvement from earlier that afternoon, it still was a huge shock to them living in such circumstances. 'You think he will come back then?'

Kitty stood up from the table and poked at the fire's glowing embers. 'Of course. We are his family. We're all he has.' She shrugged, not particularly wanting to talk about Rory. He shamed her with his faint- hearted actions. Indeed, his selfishness surprised and angered her. How could he have left them so easily? She would never forget that he'd abandoned them, but she'd forgive him.

'Maybe he's gone to the Preston family and they will help us now?' Martin said.

'I doubt it. They didn't want to help us before. Anyway, I cannot live hoping someone will come to our aid. Now, we should get some sleep. We have to look for work tomorrow.'

Kitty lingered by the dying fire after everyone was asleep. An eerie tomcat's yowl echoed out in the lane and she shivered. Without the fire's heat and light, the cold and darkness reclaimed the cellar. Somewhere above, the building creaked and groaned.

She looked around at what had become of her life. A damp, dirty cellar was all that stood between her family having a roof over their heads or being out on the streets. Emotion closed her throat and tears stung her eyes, but she was too tired and dispirited to cry. She lived in a cellar...

Chapter Four

The damp cold woke Kitty. She suffered a restless night. The creaking sounds from above as the building settled kept her from sleeping. Without a clock to tell the time, she lay awake long before she heard anyone moving from the upper floors. After donning her black woollen mourning dress, she stoked the fire and then woke Martin.

'What time is it?' he asked, rubbing sleep out of his eyes.

'I don't know. I'd say about five o'clock, though I haven't heard the knock up man yet.' She shivered and put on her coat. Having no servants to wake them at the right time, they were now dependent on the man who walked the dark streets every morning, knocking on windows of those who needed to get up and go to work. So much had changed and they had no choice but to adapt to their new life. 'Come by the fire, it's sending out some heat. I've put the kettle on to boil.'

Martin held his hands out to the flames. 'It's a good thing you know how to make a cup of tea.'

'Yes, it is, you cheeky monkey.' She raised an eyebrow at him. 'But I'll have to learn how to make proper meals too. We cannot live on sandwiches for the rest of our lives.'

'Maybe Mrs Spencer will teach you.' He put spoonfuls of sugar into his cup.

'Hey! Not so much.' She took the sugar away. 'That has to last us for some time. Everything will have to be in small amounts from now on.'

Soon, the rest awakened, complaining of hunger. With warm water heated on the fire, Kitty and Mary helped the younger ones to wash.

Footsteps above their heads signalled Kitty to pull on her gloves. 'Come, Martin, it is time to go.' She turned to Mary. 'You'll be all right. Make some breakfast and stay close to the cellar. We'll be back late this afternoon.'

She pointed her finger at Joe and Clara. 'You two help Mary look after Rosie and behave.'

At the top of the steps, they met Max.

'Good morning,' he greeted. 'What you up so early for? Bed bugs?'

Kitty shook her head as she and Martin fell into step beside him. 'I'm sure we have them, but actually we're seeking work. Do you know of any?'

'Nay, lass, there's not many who work around 'ere. Jobs are hard ter come by in these parts.'

'Where do you work?' Martin asked.

'On the river. I work in a warehouse that has its own barges. We send our stuff by river t'bigger ports along the coast.'

'Do you think there would be any chance of Martin acquiring a job there?' Kitty pushed her hands deep into her coat pockets to keep warm. 'Well, lass, it'll not hurt ter try,' Max roared, giving Martin a slap on the back. 'Come on then, lad, let's see what's up for the day.' Leaving Kitty, they strode off in the direction of the river.

Kitty stopped at the end of the lane and pondered on what to do next. Today was her twenty-first birthday. No one remembered, but that didn't matter. She was going to celebrate it by getting a job. She marched to the market full of confidence.

Even at that early hour, the market thrived with people. Stallholders set up and women shopped. Large crowds passed through the market square on their way to work in the numerous shops, factories and mills.

At each stall, Kitty inquired for work; each of the stallholders shook their heads at her. She left the market and made her way into the surrounding streets.

The first street started with a milliner's shop. She gazed at the display of colourful hats on different-sized stands. Beyond the display she saw a saleswoman dusting the counter. Smiling, Kitty entered the shop. She knew a little about hats, not the actual making of them, but she possessed a good taste of style and had worn many creations she and her mother had decorated.

The milliner gave her a firm 'no' to her enquiry of a job and told her wearing hats didn't give her the talent for making them. Chastened, and a little embarrassed, she walked on and called in at a tobacconist. The storeowner told her irritably he didn't employ women.

The streets seemed never-ending as Kitty sought employment. She was repeatedly humiliated when asked for her previous experiences and references. Of course, she had none of these and was continually turned away.

Tired and miserable, she decided to return to the cellar. She gazed with envy at the passing hansom cabs, but the less money she spent the longer they could stay out of the workhouse. Against all odds, she was determined to keep the family together and build a good life for them.

Her feet throbbed. Her stomach growled with hunger. She had eaten nothing all day and suddenly she swayed. Her head pounded and she put her hands out to lean against a brick wall. Children playing in the gutter stopped to stare at her before running off. She closed her eyes momentarily, but forced herself to walk on.

At the top of the cellar steps she hesitated, straightened her shoulders and summoned a smile. With her head held high, she went down to greet her family.

The door at the bottom was closed, properly closed. Someone had put it back on its hinges. Turning the handle, Kitty peeped in. A warm fire glowed. Mouth-watering food bubbled in a large pot on the fire's cooking shelf. A multi-coloured rag rug lay in front of the hearth. Above the mantelpiece hung a cracked mirror and on the shelf stood a tarnished carriage clock.

Walking further into the room, she saw the tidied beds and clothes packed away. A patched, cream-coloured cloth covered the old table. Where had all these things come from and where was her family?

The sound of the children's voices floated to her just before they tumbled down the cellar steps and into her outstretched arms.

Connie held back nearer to the door, watching Mary and the younger ones explain their day.

'Shh, shh! Slow down, I cannot take it all in.' Kitty laughed. 'Mary can you tell me where all this came from?' She swept her arm to encompass their new belongings.

'Yes, they're from Mrs Spencer.' Mary looked gratefully at Connie. 'She gave them to us.'

Kitty untangled herself from the little arms wrapped around her and walked over to Connie. 'Thank you so much.'

'Nay,' Connie flapped her hands, 'it were nowt, just a few bits an' pieces I 'ad spare like.'

'Will you have a cup of tea with us?'

'Er… Well…'

'Oh yes, do come and have some tea, Mrs Spencer.' Clara dimpled.

'Aye, all right then.' Connie sat at the table while Mary filled the kettle from the water pail.

Kitty listened to Connie's tone soften when she spoke to the children and saw how her gaze followed their movements with rapt attention.

Mary passed the cups around. 'Did you and Martin get work, Kitty?'

'No, I didn't,' her shoulders dropped, 'but Max took Martin to see if he can work at his warehouse.'

'If my Max can get him a job, he will.' Connie nodded.

'I know Martin has been brought up to be a gentleman and has no experience at manual work, but he's strong and intelligent.' Kitty wiped a hand over her weary eyes. So much depended on Martin getting work.

Joe laid his hand on her arm. 'Can we eat now? I'm hungry.'

Mary rounded on him. 'You do nothing but eat, Joseph McKenzie.'

'He's a growin' lad.' Connie blew on her tea to cool it. 'Go upstairs, Joe and get some more wood from my basket, there's a good lad.'

Kitty watched him go and then gazed around for signs of Rory's belongings.

Connie shook her head. 'He didn't come back, lass.'

She turned away, uncomfortable that Connie knew her thoughts. 'There's still time. Perhaps he is arranging for us to stay somewhere or even may have got work. He could become a clerk or something…'

'Aye, perhaps.' Connie's quiet murmur didn't sound convincing and Kitty winced inwardly.

Mary gripped Kitty's hands. 'This morning was awful. I put too much wood on the fire and snuffed it out. Mrs Spencer heard me crying as she went by and came down to see if I needed any help. She took us up to her rooms. We stayed by her fire while she gave us breakfast. We were so cold!

'How can I thank you, Mrs Spencer?' Kitty smiled, but tears came easily at such kindness and she hurriedly brushed them away.

'It were nowt. An' it won't be long 'til Mary has it all sorted out.' Connie gave Mary a reassuring nod. 'It'll tekk a bit of learning, that's all.'

Joe returned with the wood and threw it down with a clatter. 'We went with Mrs Spencer to a pawn shop.' His eyes widened in excitement. 'I've never been inside a pawn shop before.'

Connie sniffed. 'Well, let's hope you've no need ter go again, lad, an' stack that wood properly.'

'What about the door?' Kitty asked. 'Who did that?'

Joe looked up from his task. 'A fellow from upstairs gave us a hand when he saw us trying to fix

46

the door. He mended the hinges and put the handle on, it was his. But he said we would need it more than him.'

'A fellow?' Kitty raised her eyebrows. 'So, we have made another friend?'

'Tash McNeal lives on top floor,' Connie said. ''E's a Scot, but nice enough. His wife died two years back. We don't see him much now, keeps himself ter himself.' She turned to Mary. 'Stir the stew, Mary lass.'

Mary jumped up to obey.

Connie leaned closer to Kitty. 'You lookin' for work tomorrow?'

Kitty nodded. 'Though I think I have walked every street and lane in York. Employers turn me away because I have no experience or references.'

'You can read an' write that's what you should say t'them. It might mekk a difference.'

Kitty talked with Connie some more before they heard the booming voice of Max and the quieter undertone of Martin. Cold air blasted the room as they entered.

'Were you taken on?' Kitty asked Martin.

He grinned. 'Yes!'

Kitty jumped up to hug him, as did the others.

'I'm only a delivery boy for now, but soon I want to try and get on the boats and go to the ports along the coast.'

'I think we should take it one step at a time, yes?' Kitty laughed and hugged him again.

'Well done, lad,' Connie said.

Kitty spun to clasp Max's large hand. 'I cannot thank you enough, Max.'

'Nay, lass, it weren't my doing. The boy held his own under the supervisor's questions.'

47

'Will you stay and have supper with us?' Kitty smiled. 'You might as well, since it was your wife who cooked it.' She smiled at Connie.

Squashed around the tiny table with extra chairs brought down from the Spencer's rooms, they sat and ate the thick and tasty stew. Afterwards, Mary and Clara washed up, using the pail as a sink. Martin then went down to the tap and refilled the bucket ready for the morning.

Connie played with Rosie while Kitty and Joe helped Max construct a fireguard contraption from bits and pieces he had stored away over the years. The new fireguard meant they could buy cheap coal and keep the fire going during most of the night to keep off the chill.

In the small yard at the rear of the building, Kitty held the lantern for Max as he sorted through his treasured piles of homemade tools housed in a lean-to shed.

'I'm very grateful for you and Mrs Spencer befriending us,' Kitty said, glancing around at every small movement in the darkness.

'Think nowt of it, lass,' Max threw over his shoulder.

'I dread to imagine what might have happened to us if we didn't meet you both.'

Max straightened and faced her in the dim, brassy lantern light. 'My Connie doesn't mekk friends an' it's surprised me how she's been with your family. It pleases me ter see her so cheerful as she's been lately.' He sat on an overturned box. 'We've been married ten years an' she's allus been a loner. It's been hard for her, as she's lost many of our babbies an' it's medd her a bit defensive like. She don't know how ter show her feelings, but she's got a good heart if you willin' to look past her gruffness.'

Kitty smiled. 'She's been a Godsend, truly. I'll be her friend for as long as she wants me.'

'She's had a rough life, tekkin' care of selfish, invalid parents until they both died. She had no family but them an' so all their demands fell onto her. They wouldn't let her go out an' enjoy herself. They medd her feel guilty just for tekkin' too long at the shops.' He paused to inspect a dirty jar full of rusty bent nails. 'I were right glad ter wed her. Though, I think it took me six months ter mekk her smile.' He looked up and grinned.

Kitty returned it. 'Maybe it took her that long to realize her luck in marrying you?'

He roared with laughter. 'I like you, Kitty McKenzie.'

* * * *

Kitty pushed her way through the Christmas shoppers in the market. Women and children pressed and jostled her as she went down a narrow passage between stalls. Annoyed, she jabbed a woman in the ribs to move her bulk out of the way.

In the last four weeks, she had become accustomed to the noise and smell of the market, but every so often, she ached to visit a shop of quality like she used to with her mother. At times she dreamed of eating something light and tasty instead of the stodgy, but filling, wholesome meals Connie had shown Mary to cook. Her mouth watered at the thought of biting into a piece of chocolate or a cream-topped strawberry tart.

Huffing irritably, she dismissed the thought. It does no good thinking about what you cannot have.

However, at times, the shock of living so close to other people filled her with despondency. Hearing stranger's voices outside their little cellar window, and footsteps going over their heads at all times of the day and night drove her mad. Also, having to put up with vermin and filth everywhere was too much to face some days. The screams and arguments between people and neighbours in the lane frightened not only her, but the children too.

They saw sights of degradation and some beastly natures of men and women who used the lane for all manner of things. Abuse, neglect, and mingling with unsavoury characters was part of everyday life in the tenements. Kitty agonized over them ever leaving the bottom rung of society. Her parents would be appalled that they now lived amongst the very people her father had administered aid to.

Reaching into her pocket, she fingered the few coins there. Martin's meagre wage didn't go very far and barely bought food and coal. She tried hard not to buy more than the basic rations. However, it was difficult to live on a bland diet of scrap ends of meat, potatoes and bread after eating well all of your life.

Last night, she and Mary lowered the hems of Rosie's and Clara's dresses. Martin needed new boots, since he wore his every day for work and they showed the strains of it. She worried incessantly about their lack of money and her inability to find work.

Connie suggested the children work in the mills or factories, but Kitty refused. She wouldn't have that on her conscience. The younger children wouldn't have to slave in perilous conditions while she breathed. She was determined to make the children's lives better, but the task proved harder than she originally thought. Thank God for Connie. Without her, Kitty shuddered to think how they would be faring now.

Abruptly, Kitty stopped. A man behind bumped into her. She ignored his rude comment as she stared at the back of a tall fair-haired man. Rory. He stood at the stall on the next row. She lifted her hand, ready to call out to him, when he turned her way. The stranger stared straight past her, his face not her brother's at all.

Kitty stepped back and lowered her hand. Her heart seemed to flip against her ribs. She bit her lips to stop the tears. Her disappointment showed just how much she had missed him. Where was he? Was he safe? Where did he live? She had received no word from him and he was constantly on her mind.

She tossed her head. Tears solved nothing. Anger crept in to replace the anguish. That he could disappear without letting her know if he was all right maddened and alarmed her. When he did show his face, he would receive such a tongue lashing about his irresponsible behaviour.

'Watch out there!' A haggard chap yelled at Kitty when she stumbled into him and his wooden barrow full of carrots. 'You could've had me over with this lot then.' He struggled to keep the barrow upright.

Kitty apologized but, ignoring her, he carried on his way. A chuckle from the right drew her attention.

A bent old woman sat behind a second-hand clothing stall. 'I'd have liked t'seen him sent on his arse.'

Nodding, Kitty turned away. 'Hey, you there!'

Glancing back, Kitty frowned in surprise as the woman beckoned her over. She made certain every time she passed the market she smiled at the stallholders, in the vain hope they might offer her a job. Walking closer, she absentmindedly picked at pieces of clothing piled high on the table, not wanting to show her eagerness.

'You're called Kitty, aren't you?' 'I am, yes.'

'You allus about lookin' for work.'

'Yes.' Kitty crossed her fingers behind her back for luck.

'Would you care t'stand on this stall, for a bit of small change?'

'What exactly would you want me to do?' She didn't want to be used by the old woman, but the chance to earn a bit of money would be wonderful.

'Just t'sell me wares, that's all. Nowt hard about that.' A fit of harsh coughing wracked the woman, leaving her fighting for breath.

Horrified at such distress, Kitty hurried around to the back of the stall and eyed a pitcher of water and a mug. She poured a drink for the old woman.

'Here, thanks for that. That's why I asked you about standin' here. Some days I can hardly get outta bed.' The old woman stumbled as she stood.

Kitty put out a hand to steady her. 'I'll help you with the stall. Just tell me what I need to know.'

After five minutes of instruction, Kitty served her first customer with the old woman watching. Some items of clothing were of good quality while others were no more than rags. The piles lay jumbled on the table in no order. Customers sorted out what they wanted and usually left a messy heap afterwards.

The old woman stepped forward. 'Me name is Martha Sedgewick. You're close with Connie Spencer, aren't you?'

'Yes, we're friends.'

'My health's not good. I'll not last another winter standin' here in all weathers.'

'I'll work hard for you, Mrs Sedgewick.'

'It's six days a week. No Sundays. Every morning, you go to my lockup in the old building at the end of the market. You collect the clothes in a barrow, set up the stall and work it until half past six in the evening. At the day's end, you to pack it all away in the lock up again.'

'And my pay?'

'Eight shillings a week.'

Kitty nodded. Not a fortune, by anyone's standards, but at least it was money.

Martha waged an arthritic finger in Kitty's face. 'Don't think you can rob me either. I might be a sick old woman, but I ain't dumb.' She ambled away, bent double with coughing.

Kitty settled herself behind the stall and stood staring out at the passing traders. She had gotten herself some work at last. A silly grin wouldn't leave her face.

The wind blew up and the day turned cold. Nevertheless, the awful weather didn't deter the shoppers who only had ten days left before Christmas to do all of their buying.

Kitty was rushed off her feet attending to customers. Women rifled the contents hoping to find a good skirt or a nice blouse for the special holiday. They tossed children's clothes about looking for trousers or smocks.

Around half past two in the afternoon, a lull in customers meant Kitty finally sat on Martha's aged stool to rest her aching feet.

'Here, you can do with this I reckon.' The stallholder on Kitty's right passed her a cup of weak black tea and a slice of bread with bacon dripping smeared on it.

'Why, thank you.' Kitty's stomach rumbled in response and she blushed. 'It's very much appreciated.'

'I'm Iris Nettlesmith.' She indicated her stall. 'I've got household bits and pieces.'

'Pleased to meet you, I'm Kitty McKenzie.'

Iris looked her up and down. 'You're not our sort, are you lass? You speak posh like.'

Kitty swallowed. 'I live in a cellar in a tenement building in Walmgate, Mrs Nettlesmith. I think that now makes me one of you.'

Iris chuckled. 'Well, lass, if you work as hard as you've done this morning, you'll do all right for me.'

Come six o'clock, Martha Sedgewick hobbled back to the stall. She stared at the money tin in surprise. 'You've been busy.'

'Yes.' Kitty waited, hoping the old woman would be pleased.

Iris sauntered over to them. 'Kitty's lovely face an' pleasant way of speaking medd folk buy more than they wanted, an' they weren't even aware of it.'

Martha peered around the stall and nodded. 'You'll do I suppose.'

'Then you'll take me on every day?' Kitty sagged in relief. She started to put the clothes in the barrow, her feet aching.

'Nay, lass, I'll do it. Get yourself home.'

Ridiculous tears blurred her vision. 'Thank you, Mrs Sedgewick. You won't regret hiring me, I promise.'

Chapter Five

The next day, Kitty hurried to the market even before Max and Martin left for the warehouse. In the silver light of dawn, she slid open the lockup door. Large crates, piled high with all types of second-hand and warehouse-damaged stock, filled the room. She took her time and chose the better pieces. Gazing around, she frowned at the untidiness of the place. Obviously, the crates had not been sorted for months. Instead, someone had dumped each new collection of clothes on top of the other crates. A strong urge to stay and arrange things made her clench her hands in frustration. However, she had a stall to run and if she didn't hurry Martha would think she wasn't coming.

Her second day proved just as busy and once again she ate lunch on her feet. Throughout the day, she and Iris chatted and laughed. The feeling of well-being and Christmas cheer rang throughout the market.

When Martha came in the evening to pick up the day's takings, she nodded in approval at Kitty's effort.

Kitty paused in folding and putting away the clothes. 'May I have a moment before you go, Mrs Sedgewick?'

'Aye.'

'Would...' She drew in a breath. 'Would it be possible for me to put the stall in some kind of order?' she asked cautiously.

'What do you mean?' Martha frowned.

'Well, I think if the stall looked tidier, more people would wish to come over and look at it. It would attract them.'

Martha angrily jabbed her finger at her. 'You've only been here two minutes an' you're tryin' t'tell me how t'run me stall?'

'No, no, please let me explain.' She wished she had kept her big mouth shut. 'I'm simply trying to make the stall look better which in turn will make you more money.'

Iris, on hearing the exchange, came over and nudged Martha. 'You've never medd that kinda money in two days before, so she must 'ave somethin' in that pretty head of hers.' Iris folded her arms across her bony chest.

Martha scratched her chin. 'Aye, well, I suppose it wouldn't hurt t'try, but I'm tellin' you, if all this carryon means a drop in customers then you're out.' Martha stared hard at her before turning back to continue counting her money.

Iris nodded and winked at Kitty.

After Martha left, Kitty packed the wooden barrow, said goodnight to Iris and the other stallholders and wheeled the barrow to the lockup. Inside, she lit a candle in a holder she had borrowed from Iris. Its soft glow made the room seem warmer than it truly was. Kitty took off her coat and gloves and began pulling out clothes from the crates.

Soon, six ever-growing heaps surrounded her— men's, women's, boy's, girl's and baby's clothes.

Ruined clothes became rag bundles sold for halfpenny a pound weight.

Kitty lost track of time while she sorted. The door banged open, echoing in the cold room, and she nearly jumped out of her skin.

A seedy-looking man, with greasy hair poking out beneath a dirty flat cap, stood in the doorway. He wore a soiled green jacket and a brown pair of trousers that looked like they'd never seen water and soap.

He smirked, revealing several missing teeth. 'What have we got here then?'

Straightening, she raised her eyebrow in contempt. 'Who may you be, sir?'

'I was gonna ask you the same question, Missie.' His small beady eyes narrowed.

'I have every right to be here. I work for Mrs Sedgewick. So be off with you.'

'Martha never told me 'owt about hirin' somebody. What's your name, then?'

'That is no concern of yours.' She looked past him into the empty square beyond. He seemed harmless but he also blocked the only exit.

Scratching his head under his cap, he peered around. 'Me name's Kip. I'm about t'mekk you piles there even bigger.'

Kitty raised her chin in disapproval. 'I beg your pardon?'

Kip grinned before disappearing into the darkness outside only to return a few minutes later carrying a box of clothes. He unceremoniously dumped it at her feet. Looking from the clothes to Kitty, he laughed. 'How did you think Martha got about getting all this lot? It doesn't come here by itself.'

She bent down and looked through the new additions, all ladies skirts and blouses in quite good condition. She held up a pretty blue blouse. The garments in this crate were of better quality than the others. 'I started working for her two days ago.'

'How is the old bird?'

'Not too good. That is why I'm working her stall.'

'Why in hell's name are you nosin' about in here at this time of night?' He leaned against the doorways and retrieved his pipe and tobacco from his jacket pocket.

'Trying to sort out the mess. I think the stall can look better with a bit of organization.'

'Aye, well, the poor old girl is gettin' beyond doin' anythin' like that,' Kip murmured, as white-yellow smoke drifted around his head.

There was movement behind Kip, and Kitty saw Max's big frame come into the weak candlelight.

'Kitty?' Max's voice boomed out over Kip's shoulder, making the younger man drop the pipe out of his mouth.

She reassured him with a smile. 'I'm all right.'

Max shouldered past Kip. 'We were worried. I came t'look for you.'

'I'm sorry to worry you. I didn't mean to be so long.' Kitty patted his arm. 'I have done enough for one day.'

'I'll lock the door when I'm finished.' Kip stepped back from the door to let them through.

She paused. 'How do I know I can trust you?'

He laughed. 'If I don't deliver the goods I don't get paid.'

'They aren't stolen, are they?'

Kip made a cross over his heart and winked. 'I swear on my mother's soul.'

Taking her elbow, Max led her outside and whispered, 'I doubt he even has a mother.'
Chuckling, Kitty tiredly walked home.

* * * *

Flakes of snow drifted on the breeze and fell to the ground, within seconds they melted. The sun, although weak, shone between fluffy clouds. The children, being children, wanted snow for Christmas.

Kitty preferred it not to snow at all as she stood behind the stall table gazing at the display with pride, before turning her attention to a customer.

Iris, cup of tea in hand, strolled over and watched her wrap a pair of boy's trousers in brown paper and tie it with string. 'Martha won't believe 'er eyes,' she repeated for the umpteenth time that morning.

Kitty gave the package to the customer, took the money and thanked her. Turning to Iris, she smiled. 'I'm glad you like it. People are coming over to look.' She picked up a discarded skirt, folded it neatly, and placed it back on the pile again.

She'd spent a great deal of time that morning arranging the table. With Iris's help, she managed to find some wire and threaded it along the front of the stall. There, she hung the best garments. Along the back of the stall and down its supports, she strung little girls' dresses and eye- catching shawls for women. On the table, she placed neat rows of folded clothes starting with men's clothes at the back, and then going down in size to babies at the front. Regular customers noticed the overall transformation and couldn't resist coming closer to take a proper look.

At the end of the day, Martha counted the money.

'Are you happy with the changes?' She hoped Martha would be pleased.

'Aye.'

'I have some more ideas, if you would like to listen to them.'

'You can do what you like. Money's up on past Christmas Eves,' Martha told her without looking up.

'I'm pleased about that.' Kitty smiled. 'Only, the other ideas will need to have a little money spent.'

At this, Martha's head shot up. 'What do you mean, money spent?'

'Well, I would like to obtain better stands for the clothes to hang from and some good hangers. I thought we could hang dresses inside the stall at the back so women can see them in full. Maybe we—'

'Now, just hang on a minute!' Martha slammed the tin lid down. 'I know you come from a background with plenty of money, but your fancy ways won't do for about here. Who do you think has brass in their pockets t'spend on fancy dresses that go on hangers?'

Kitty, worried she'd pushed Martha too far, remained quiet. She didn't want to lose her job the day before Christmas and especially after all her hard work. She waited until the other woman caught her breath, then apologized.

Martha turned away muttering and picked up the tin. She opened it and took out some coins then closed the lid again. Turning back to Kitty, she held out her hand. 'Here's your money.'

With a sinking heart, Kitty accepted the money. After a second glance at the amount she realized Martha had given her too much. 'Martha you gave me twelve shillings.'

'Aye, that's right.'

Kitty gazed from the money in her hand to Martha. Terror choked her. 'Have…have I lost my job?'

'Lost your job?' Martha frowned. 'What you talkin' about? Of course you haven't. You've done well, so you've got a Christmas bonus and you can tekk what clothes you want for the children.'

Kitty closed her eyes briefly in relief. 'Thank you.'

'I'll see you in a few days. Good Christmas to you.' Martha nodded to Iris, who listened in on their conversation, and then shuffled away home.

Winter darkness descended with another flurry of snow. Speedily, Kitty packed away the clothes. Other stallholders did the same, while shouting out Merry Christmas to each other.

'Well, Iris, I'm finished for the day. I want to get home to the children.' Kitty loaded up the barrow. She kept a blue blouse aside, intending it to be Connie's Christmas present. Connie wore the same few articles of clothing week in week out. She never spent money on herself.

'Did you tekk some clothes for the bairns?'

'No, I don't wish to be greedy. I just selected a blouse for my friend, as a thank you for all her help.'

'Listen lass, Martha won't offer again til next Christmas, if she lasts that long. So, tekk what you want while you got the chance.'

Kitty bit her lip. 'Do you think she is that ill?'

Iris nodded. 'Aye, I do. Her chest is awful bad an' she's got all winter t'get through yet.' Iris came closer. 'If I were you, lass, I'd see if she'd let you buy this stall.' Iris raised her eyebrows. 'Get somethin' down on paper soon, else you'll be out of a job.'

On the way home, Kitty's head rang with Iris's ominous words. She pondered them during the evening as she helped the children put up colourful paper chains around the cellar. Iris was right and she needed to act, but how could she buy the stall? It took all her money and Martin's just to live. There was nothing spare for the future.

Max managed to arrange a small Christmas tree for them and the children decorated it. Underneath it, they placed the small presents Kitty had bought.

'You seem a little down in't mouth tonight, lass. Is summat wrong?' Connie asked, holding Rosie on her knee.

'I'm fine.' Kitty poured another cup of tea. She didn't want to tell Connie about her fears concerning Martha and the stall and spoil the evening's mood. Besides, she might be worrying for no reason at all.

It was routine now for Max and Connie to come down each night to share a cup of tea with her and the children. In fact, Connie spent nearly all her time in the cellar. During the day she stayed with Mary and the young ones, teaching them about life in the tenements and showing Mary how to make filling dinners out of nothing much at all. On weekends, if the weather was fine enough, they took the children out for walks and played games.

'I know it must be hard, this bein' your first Christmas away from home,' Connie whispered, not letting the others hear.

'Yes, but we'll survive it.' Kitty stirred her tea. 'I want the children to be happy and to not dwell on the festivities of their other Christmases. We miss our parents and sister Davina. However, it could've been much worse if we hadn't met you.'

'Nay, you'd 'ave managed. You're tougher then you think.' Connie nodded at her. She gave Rosie a loving squeeze, then let the little girl scramble down off her knee to go and look at the Christmas tree. 'I can honestly say, lass, you've medd me an' Max the happiest couple in York. I can't imagine me life without you in it. Me life was so lonely before you lot came and I didn't even know it.'

Kitty took her hand and smiled. Connie had never spoken so privately to her before. Their friendship grew more each day and Kitty was thankful for she, like Connie, had never known a true friend.

'For us, this Christmas will be the best we've 'ad,' Connie continued.

'Our Christmases were always full of noise and visitors,' Kitty recalled, 'and you know, I never really enjoyed them. We never had Christmas with just us children around the tree on Christmas morning. Oh no, mother would consider that a failure. She always invited half of their friends for Christmas Day, and the other half for the day after.' Kitty shrugged and sighed. 'We children were usually cast aside in favour of the guests. Mother never realized she was treating us that way. She thought, as long as the nursery was stocked full of toys then we would be happy, but I never was.'

'It's funny 'ow two lives can be so different, yet just t'same,' murmured Connie, staring into the fire embers.

* * * *

Christmas Day dawned cold and rainy. Kitty threw back the covers and put on her coat, slipped her feet into an old pair of slippers and padded to the fireplace. Cinders winked between the ashes.

Carefully, she put on small bits of wood, blowing gently until it caught alight. Satisfied the fire would burn, she put the kettle on to boil and placed the frying pan next to it. By the time the children staggered out of bed, the flames licked the back of the chimney and a delightful smell of frying bacon scented the cellar.

'Can we open our presents now?' Clara asked, eyeing her breakfast. 'No, we'll wait for Connie and Max to come down.' Kitty bent to kiss her on the cheek. 'There's warm water in the bowl by the fire. Give yourself a wash and help Rosie wash too.'

Mary tidied their beds. 'Joe, can you go down to the tap and get some more water, please?'

Joe sighed dramatically. 'Can it wait?'

'No.' Mary tucked in a blanket. 'The sooner you do it, the sooner we open our gifts.'

Kitty grinned as she brewed the tea. After living like this for six weeks they were slowly accepting the change. Admittedly, at first the children had expected all to be as before and living without servants had been an unpleasant change, but now they knew this was their way of life for the time being. If Rory still lived with them, they would have three wages coming in. With three wages they could leave the cellar and rent rooms elsewhere. Daily, she expected him to knock on the door and humbly ask for their forgiveness. The children missed him, their handsome brother, and receiving no word from him hurt. Yet, beyond that, fury ruled over the pain.

All week she had believed he would return for Christmas, if only to stay for five minutes. Yet each day, her hope dwindled a little more. However, it did no good to dwell on such things. Talking about him had become a taboo subject.

65

She sighed and glanced at the door, expecting it to open and Rory to stand there. He would come today—it was Christmas. Kitty looked at the clock. There was time yet.

Max's booming voice caused a stir among the children as he descended the steps. In great excitement, they opened the door to him and Connie. With a bellow almost lifting the ceiling, he hugged them close before hoisting Rosie into the air. Next, he led them into singing Christmas carols as he placed small parcels under the tree.

Kitty sidestepped Max and her laughing siblings to take Connie's hand and admire the blue blouse she gave her the day before. 'Merry Christmas. You look lovely.' She kissed Connie's cheek and grinned when the other woman blushed.

'Aye, thank you, lass. Happy Christmas. Now, I've got the goose cookin' upstairs, it'll be a while though. I'll go up an' put the vegetables on later. Do you go t'church today?'

'Er… No, not really. We always went at Christmas and Easter, but on most Sundays, Mother and Father rose rather late due to arriving home in the early hours from social outings. I thought it was a bit hypocritical only attending sometimes.' Kitty shrugged. 'I'm afraid I haven't made much effort since they died.'

'Never mind. Max and I aren't that close ter God either. I lost my faith long ago.'

'I must try harder, at least for the children.'

Connie sniffed. 'Apparently, God forgives us weaker followers.'

'Are you sure?' She frowned. 'He may think I don't deserve to join Him.'

'Eh, lass, you the limit.' Connie laughed.

Looking up at the sound, Max smiled. 'That's the ticket, me lass. Let us laugh all day.'

'Right then,' Kitty announced. 'I think it's time we opened the presents.'

* * * *

All too quickly, the holidays finished. The new year of eighteen hundred and sixty-five ushered in bad weather; snow fell and lay in thick drifts. Old timers said they felt this winter would be dire and the mood of the city seemed to reflect this. People swearing and cursing at each other replaced the happy Christmas cheer. In the bitter cold, tempers flared. It seemed no one had a kind word for anyone.

Together, Kitty and Iris sat behind their stalls warming their hands in front of a small fire lit each day inside a large iron bucket. Half of the bucket had been cut away and the other half had holes in it. The basic contraption kept the worst of the cold away.

As trade dropped due to the wretched weather, Kitty had more time to think of Rory. He hadn't turned up at Christmas, disappointing them all. Her heart hardened towards him at his thoughtlessness. She couldn't believe he was so selfish.

By the end of the first week in January, Kitty needed more coats to sell. Hugging herself to keep warm, she waited until Martha finished counting the coins in the tin. 'Martha, we're low on scarves and coats—' The old woman's wracking cough stopped her and she rushed to help the old woman.

'K…Kip's comin' tomorrow,' Martha said between coughs. She stumbled away, hunched over and gasping for breath.

Kitty shook her head. Each day Martha became more ill.

''Ave you asked her about t'stall?' inquired Iris.

'No, not yet.' Kitty sighed. 'I'll talk to her soon.'

The following morning, Kitty traipsed through the snow to the market place. She hated how the snow covered things that tripped you if you didn't hold your skirts high and tread carefully. A few stallholders grouped together nodded to her and then glanced away. She picked her way over squashed frozen fruit, glad that for once the over-ripe fruit smell didn't linger throughout the square.

Nearer to the lock up, she saw the huge door was open. Alarm sent her heart racing. Hurrying across the icy cobbles, Kitty skidded to the doorway. She stared at the yawning space that, just last night, was filled with bulging crates. A ripple of fear tingled down her back.

Someone had robbed them.

Kitty dithered on the spot for a moment, unsure what to do. She bit her lip and begged her mind to think straight. Out of the corner of her eye, she noticed someone coming towards her.

Iris pulled Kitty's arm and thrust her into the lockup, closing the door behind them.

'Iris—'

'Listen to me,' Iris demanded as Kitty started to babble. 'Martha is dead.'

The words struck her like a physical blow. 'W-What? Oh no.'

'They found 'er last evenin'. I came across them standin' around 'er when I was on me way home. I called for the doctor an' once 'e came, I left t'go home. But, I did manage t'get this.' Iris pushed the stall's money tin into her hands.

Kitty stepped back, horrified. 'I…I cannot have this.'

'Now, listen an' think 'ard.' Iris shook Kitty's shoulder. 'This is all you gonna get, 'cos a fella called Kip came, an' when 'e found out she was dead 'e took all the clothes. 'E said it all belonged to 'im. So, now you've got nowt. No job.'

Kitty sagged. 'I knew something was going to happen. I could just feel it. It was too good to be true.' Misery welled inside her, sapping her strength.

'I told yer to get something down on paper, didn't I?' She nodded miserably.

Iris leaned closer. 'I've an idea if you want t'listen to it?'

'Yes?'

'Somewhere in Martha's 'ouse she's stashed all 'er money. I rekkon you should go an' nab it.' Iris's eyes grew wide with enthusiasm.

Kitty reared away as though struck. 'I could never do that! It's stealing.'

Iris shook her again. 'If you don't, then someone else will. Her place will be picked over before nightfall.'

'Yes, well, those people will have it on their conscience and most probably will be caught too.'

Iris snorted and walked to the door. Opening it, she looked over her shoulder. 'I told you about it cos I thought you could use it for the bairns, that's all.'

Dazed, Kitty trudged back to the cellar. The cold seeped into her boots, freezing her toes, but that was the least of her worries.

At the top of the cellar steps, she met Connie and Mary taking the children out to the shops.

Connie took her arm. 'Lass, what you doing home?'

'Martha has died. The stall is no more. The clothes are gone.' Kitty went down and sat at the table without taking off her coat or gloves. She dumped the money tin on the table. It repulsed her.

Connie, sensing her despair, nodded to Mary to go without her. With the children gone, Connie stoked the fire up and put the kettle on to boil. 'I'm so sorry, lass.' She placed teacups on the table. 'Hard-luck stories are more than common in this part of the world.'

'What am I to do, Connie?' Kitty folded her arms on the table. She tried to swallow her tears but the emotion was too great and she put her head down to cry.

'Nay, lass, don't tekk on so.' Connie patted her back. 'Summat will come along. You've still got Martin in work an' you know Max an' me will help.'

'I'm tired of struggling,' she mumbled between sobs. 'I cannot do it anymore.'

'You've had a setback, lass, we all do. I know it's hard for you, you're not used to it, but struggling is what I've done all me life. You'll be right again in no time.'

Kitty jerked up. 'I don't want to be right again. I want to go home.' She flung her arms out wide. 'I hate this cellar. I hate my parents for ruining my life and I hate Rory for leaving us.' Sobs tore at her throat. She couldn't breathe.

Connie stood and gathered her into an embrace. 'I know, lass, I know.'

Finally spent, Kitty allowed Connie to sit her back down. 'I'm sorry.'

Connie tutted. 'What tosh. You've nowt ter be sorry about.' She pushed the teacup closer. 'Have a drink, lass.'

Kitty clasped her hand. 'What would I do without you and Max?'

'Well, we're not plannin' on goin' anywhere, lass.' Connie patted her hand.

Chapter Six

Kitty sat at the table perusing the employment column in the newspaper as she had done every week for a month. A heavy fall of snow forced the children to stay inside. Near the fire, Connie and Mary darned socks while listening to Clara and Joe take turns in reading aloud pages from Robinson Crusoe. At their feet, Rosie played on the mat with a rag doll.

A tap sounded at the door. They all stopped to stare at each other. 'Whoever knocks at our door?' Joe said, lowering the book.

Standing and automatically straightening her skirts, Kitty put a hand to her hair, a habit ingrained since birth, and went to open the door.

A tall gentleman stood on the cellar steps. He wore a long coat made of wool of deepest black. No hat adorned his head and snowflakes glistened on his shiny blue-black hair.

'Good afternoon.'

Staring, Kitty inclined her head. 'Good afternoon.'

'I'm looking for a Miss Kitty McKenzie. I was told she lived in this…lane.'

'I am she.'

From inside his coat, he pulled out a roll of papers and handed them to Kitty. 'I deliver you these documents on behalf of Mrs Martha Sedgewick, deceased.'

Stunned, Kitty hesitated to take them from him. Her experience with documents in the past had never been kind. 'W…what are they?'

'A copy of her last will, made just before Christmas. In it she states she has no kin and she leaves all her worldly goods to you.'

Kitty gazed at him. His beautiful cornflower-blue eyes, fringed with thick black lashes, stared at her and when he smiled, her heart thumped against her ribs. Her body tingled with awareness. She wasn't sure if it was because of him or the news he just gave her, but for some reason her legs shook.

Behind her, Connie rose. 'I'm Mrs Spencer. Would you care t'come in an' stand by the fire for a minute? T'weather is dreadful.'

He looked around the cellar before glancing from Connie to Kitty. He frowned, but nodded. If he was surprised to find one of his own living in such conditions, he did well not to comment on it.

'Would you care for a cup of tea? We've milk an' sugar.' Connie sat Kitty down.

His expression changed from puzzlement to a warm smile. The softer expression was more natural, handsome, and not so formidable and it took Kitty's breath away. 'A cup of tea would be most welcome. Thank you.'

Kitty gestured to the table, and then hid her hands in her lap to disguise her trembling. He smelt wonderfully clean and fresh. His white collar, stiffly starched, glowed bright against the dimness of the cellar. Her stomach clenched and she had an urge to just sit and stare at him forever. 'Please, sit down, Mr?' She glanced up at him.

'Forgive me, my name is Kingsley. Benjamin Kingsley.'

'Are you Martha's solicitor?'

'No. However, her solicitor contacted my family concerning her affairs.' He studied the children and their surroundings.

Kitty assumed he wondered at their background, but was too well mannered to ask.

'So, you're Martha's family, Mr Kingsley?' Connie probed deeper, pouring boiling water into the teapot.

Kingsley smiled. 'No, though we do have a connection with her. You see, a long time ago, she was my grandfather's...er...friend. On his deathbed, I promised him I'd help her should she ever have need. She never did ask for help and so I thought the least I could do was to make certain her will was taken care of properly.'

Connie snorted. 'Good lord, I wouldn't have thought Martha as the mistress type.'

'Connie!' admonished Kitty, although the information stunned her too.

'It's all right.' Kingsley grinned. 'I wouldn't have thought so either, but they say that she was quite a beauty as a young woman. Obviously, she caught the eye of my grandfather.'

'Why didn't he marry her?' Mary murmured, always the romantic.

'Because, I'm ashamed to say...he was already married.'

At that, they were all quiet.

Forcing herself to concentrate, Kitty read the documents until Kingsley interrupted her.

'Have you lived here long?'

She glanced up. His handsome features started a fluttering in her stomach of a kind she'd not known before. It was as though her body had control over her and all intelligence had deserted her. 'Over three months.'

He nodded. For an instant, a look of sympathy stole across his handsome face. 'It is very different to what you are used to?'

She couldn't help but smile. Did they not appear as though they always lived here? At times it felt like it. 'Indeed.'

Kingsley stood and glanced down at her. His eyes darkened and his lips curved into a knee-knocking smile. 'I must be going now.'

'Of course,' she agreed, but inside, her heart said no, not yet. He was her kind, and for a little bit longer she wanted to pretend she still belonged to his world.

He turned to Connie and handed her the cup. 'Thank you very much for the tea, Mrs Spencer.' He headed for the door.

Joe got there first and opened it for him. 'You've a coat like my Papa used to own.'

He paused to put his hand on Joe's head and chuckled. 'Then your Papa must have possessed fine taste, lad.'

'He did. He was a doctor.'

'Really?' Kingsley frowned as if in thought.

Kitty pulled Joe to her. 'Enough, Joe. Let the gentleman be on his way.'

Benjamin Kingsley took her hand and bowed over it. 'Good afternoon to you, Miss McKenzie.'

'And to you, Mr Kingsley, and thank you.'

'Oh, I nearly forgot.' He rummaged in his trouser pocket and pulled out a key. 'Martha's key. After you have collected what you want, I'd be obliged if you could return the key to Jarret and Hunters, Solicitors, in Coney Street.'

'Thank you, I will.' She smiled.

His gaze locked with hers. 'If you have need of me, leave word at Coney Street.'

Kitty swallowed and nodded, letting her imagination believe he hinted at something more than he implied. Embarrassed by her wayward thoughts, she blushed and ducked her head. What had come over her? She'd never been the kind who wanted a man's sole attention. She was acting such a fool.

'Keep well.' He held up his hand in a final goodbye to everyone, before running lightly up the cellar steps.

Reluctantly closing the door behind him, Kitty wondered if she'd ever see him again and hoped that she would. Kingsley had been a reminder of the past, dressed in the image of her father, and his presence in their alien world had returned her to the other life she'd once lived, if only for a short time.

Connie tidied away their cups. 'That was kind of him, comin' 'ere personally like. His type don't often go out of their way for others and they never enter this part of the city.'

'Yes, it was kind.' Sighing, she turned over the key in her hand. 'I just don't believe it. Who would have thought?'

'Imagine old Martha bein' a wealthy gent's mistress!' Connie's eyes grew wide in surprise.

'What's a mistress?' Clara asked.

'Never mind,' Kitty said quickly.

'You best get over ter Martha's place before dark.' Connie put her hands on her hips. 'Though I doubt there'll be much left by now.'

'I don't understand why she left her things to me?'

'She knew you t'be a good person, that's why, an' you're in need.'

Kitty looked at the key again. 'I don't think I can do it. It's like stealing. I mean… Well, it doesn't feel right to go picking about somebody else's belongings. Besides, I didn't know her that well. I still have her money tin. Surely—'

'Stop your nonsense.' Connie went to the back of the door, took her old thin coat off the hook as well as Kitty's coat and gave it to her. 'She wanted you t'ave it!'

'But, Connie…'

'Oh, come on with you. You get nowt for nowt in this life. You worked hard for her an' she's rewardin' you.'

'I did receive a wage,' she protested.

Connie tutted and steered Kitty up the cellar steps.

* * * *

Martha had rented rooms in an old grand house made into flats, just like all the other Georgian houses in the street. The houses no longer presented the splendour of their former years. Paint peeled away at the slightest touch. Most of the windows, the ones not broken, had no kind of drapery hanging behind them. Nothing showed that the residents took the least care of their homes in this part of town. Rubbish littered the street, the wind having piled it in places like dirty ant nests. Half-starved dogs and cats roamed. Every now and then, they erupted into fighting masses of fur and made a hideous noise.

Few of the huge trees that once proudly lined the street remained, many being cut up for firewood. The rest stood deformed and broken, their lower branches gone. Even the snow, sitting in deep drifts against the walls, looked grimy in the dullness of winter's gloom.

Kitty hesitated as they approached the building, uneasy about entering the dead woman's home.

A loud bang shattered the stillness of the late afternoon. As it echoed, a bloodcurdling scream came from somewhere behind the soot-covered walls.

'What the 'ell was that?' Connie whispered, clutching Kitty's arm.

'Let us go back.' Kitty turned to go. The last month she had walked the streets every day looking for work to no avail, and it was getting harder and harder to survive on Martin's meagre wages. However, nothing Martha owned was worth putting herself or Connie in danger.

'No. We're here now, let's just get on with it.' Connie led the way into the hall.

Kitty sighed and, gathering her black skirts, followed.

The numbers on the doors indicated they must go upstairs. Once they reached the next landing, they saw some of the doors didn't have numbers.

Connie, taking the bull by the horns as usual, knocked on the first door.

A woman, holding a child on her hip, answered. 'Aye?'

'We're after old Martha Sedgewick's rooms.' Connie sniffed.

'She's dead.'

'Aye, we know that.' Connie huffed. 'It's 'er rooms we want. Do you know them or not?'

The woman shifted the child up higher and pointed to the door opposite.

'Ta, very much.' Connie nodded to the woman, took Kitty's elbow and drew her to the other door.

Nervously, Kitty put the key in the lock and opened the door. The dim room smelled musty. A fireplace and a cooking range lined the far wall. A door to the left led to a small, airless bedroom; it contained an iron bed and an old chest of drawers.

Connie opened each of the four drawers and found a few pieces of clothing.

'Well, the bed an' drawers will come in handy.' Connie sniffed again. 'You know, I don't think anyone's been here.'

'Maybe they had someone keeping an eye on the place?' They went back into the main room to search more closely.

Kitty indicated to an utterly filthy horsehair sofa looking well past its use. 'We aren't taking that.'

A small, round table stood in the middle of the room with only two chairs. On the wall hung a painting of a small cottage set amongst fields in the countryside. Kitty liked it and took it down from its nail, leaving a square-shaped outline a lighter colour than the rest of the smoke-stained wall.

'She didn't have much, did she?' Kitty lay the painting on the table.

Connie searched through some cupboards near the fireside. She took out a tea service in fine bone china with a pretty pattern of pink roses on it. 'Look 'ere. This is an attractive set.'

'Oh yes, that is lovely, much better than ours.' She would never get used to the ugly crockery they used in the cellar.

'This cabinet is what you need for all your things.' Connie ran her hands over the cabinet's wooden surface. 'I can't believe 'tis all still here,' she added in disbelief.

'It's here,' a voice said from the doorway, 'cos a toff said he'd have us all arrested if we touched any of it.'

Spinning around, Connie and Kitty stared at the woman from across the hall. She leaned against the doorjamb with her baby placed at her feet.

'Well, what surprises me is you took any notice,' Connie muttered with a snort.

'Me ol' man's already down the line. I'll not be joinin' him.' The woman gave a cheerless laugh. 'Besides, men kept a good eye on't place.' Without saying any more, she picked up the baby and went back to her own door.

'I still feel as though I'm stealing,' Kitty murmured, closing the door after the woman.

'I told you, she wanted you ter have it. She knew you were struggling and that you had a family ter support.'

'But I hardly knew her.'

'Well, you must've medd a good impression in a short time then.'

Kitty walked over to the cooking range and picked up a few of the pots dangling on hooks above it. They'd be useful. On a shelf to the right of the range stood a few items of food. A jar of currants and a small bottle of pickles, plus a marble slab that held a chunk of dreadfully smelling cheese and some shrivelled up salty beef. Indeed, it made her sad to see that a woman of Martha's age had very little to show for all those years.

She heard Connie banging about in the other room and went to investigate. In the bedroom, Connie had flipped the bed over on its side and banged on the floorboards underneath.

'What are you doing?'

Connie sat back on her haunches. 'She's bound t'ave some money stashed away somewhere.'

'Oh, good heavens. I feel like a grave robber. Put that bed down this minute! We are going. I've had enough.' She spun on her heel.

Connie followed her out. 'I'm tellin' you it's worth lookin' about a bit.'

'No.'

'Lass, you going t'need every bit of it.'

Kitty spun to face Connie. 'Why are you so sure she has some money hidden away? She was a woman who sold second-hand clothes on a stall all her life! What makes you think she has hordes of money somewhere?'

'Cos it mekks sense, that's why! Iris Nettlesmith has had a stall beside Martha for forty years. She knows Martha has done some good trade over the years, but it never showed that she spent much of it. She never had no family ter spend it on. So, the money must have gone somewhere.'

'I doubt it.'

Connie put her hand to her head and sighed. 'Who knows, mebbe Kingsley's grandfather gave her money? It won't do any harm ter look now, will it?'

'Five more minutes and then we go home and forget all about it.' Kitty took off her coat. She went to the other room and began to press on the floorboards. Connie pulled at the bed and then looked for secret compartments in the chest of drawers and the cabinet. After an hour of pushing and prodding, turning and picking up anything not nailed down, they gave up.

'I told you so,' said Kitty through the dust they'd stirred up in the room.

Connie banged her fist on the table. 'It's here somewhere, I can feel it.'

Kitty chuckled. 'Come on, it is almost dark.'

She reached for her coat and gloves resting on the back of the sofa.

One of the gloves fell to the floor and, bending to pick it up, something caught her eye. The sofa material was a dark olive green, but the fabric on the back looked newer than the rest. The stitching around the entire back part of the sofa was in a different shade.

Intrigued, she knelt and pulled at a loose thread. Swiftly the thread unravelled, the material fell away from the sofa. Kitty glanced up at Connie, who watched fascinated. Lifting the material flap revealed the wooden structure, and, at the bottom, a box nailed onto a small shelf on the base.

'Oh my.' Kitty held her breath as she reached in and raised the box's lid. Gently, she lifted out a little velvet bag. Within it came the soft clink of coins rubbing together. Handing the bag to Connie, Kitty stretched in again and kept doing so until the box was empty.

They stood at the table and stared in wonderment at thirty-two bags. 'I...I never expected to find anything,' Kitty whispered.

'The jammy old sod.' Connie grunted. 'She lived like a pauper an' yet had all this.'

'Oh, Connie, I cannot take this money. It's not right.' The pile of bags made her queasy. She looked nervously over her shoulder at the door, expecting the police to come barging through any minute and arrest her for trespassing.

Connie gave her a sharp jab with her finger. 'Listen, lass, I know you don't feel right about it. But when you think about it, who else is goin' ter have it? She's got no kin.'

Speechless, Kitty shook her head.

Connie picked up the first bag, opened it and tipped out the coins onto the table. In a short time, the coins were stacked into small towers. Each bag contained ten gold sovereigns totalling three hundred and twenty.

'Oh, lass,' Connie whispered wide-eyed.

* * * *

Flames licked the coal in the fireplace. The children's chests rose lightly as they slept peacefully in their beds.

Kitty sat at the table staring at the bags of coins in front of her. They would change her life and she wasn't sure whether she was ready for that to happen again. Unbelievably, the cellar had become their home and although it was damp, the walls ran with slime and the rats tried to eat everything in sight, they had grown used to it. The children played in the lane outside and made friends with the other children. Joe and Clara attended a nearby school. Mary worked hard at keeping the cellar clean and comfortable as well as learning to cook, just as Martin worked solidly at earning a wage for them. They also had the friendship and support of the Spencers. She was frightened to leave the relative security of the cellar to face the unknown again.

What is the best option now?

Kitty slumped in the chair and sighed deeply. The money meant they could afford to live in a nice place and wear good quality clothes again. With careful management, they might live well for a year or two.

Yes, finding the money was a Godsend, but somehow it didn't give her the pleasure it should. Decisions overwhelmed her, throwing her into a pit of despair. The whole process of packing up and moving away and starting again filled her with dread. Where would they go? She didn't want to have to do it all again just yet. Outside of the cellar the world was cold and lonely and frightening.

The coal shifted in the grate. Kitty yawned and reached over to idly pick up the newspaper. Flicking through the pages, she barely read a word. Tiredness made her limbs heavy, her mind sluggish, but she knew she wouldn't sleep, not properly. Halfway through the paper, something stopped her from turning the page. A story heading leapt out at her, Tales From The Colony, Kitty read what followed. On finishing the article, she rested the paper on her knee and stared into the flames of the fire. Somewhere in the recesses of her mind a memory came to her.

Her parents hosted a dinner party. One guest had just returned from the southern colonies of Australia and New Zealand. Throughout the evening, he told stories of his adventures and Kitty remembered how he kept everyone spellbound by his tales, especially her. For days afterwards, she spent hours in their library reading books about those countries, hoping she could one day visit them. The gentleman's account intrigued her still.

The clock's chimes brought Kitty out of her reverie. She put the paper on the table and then banked the fire down for the night. While placing the fireguard up and blowing out the candles, her mind came alive with plans. By the time she climbed into bed, the decision was made.

Chapter Seven

'Australia!' Max and Connie spoke as one.

Kitty sipped her tea. 'Yes, a new start for all of us.'

'B…but why there?' Connie spluttered. 'Why go t'other side of the world?'

'Because I think it would be good for us. The children could do very well in a new country. There is a lot of opportunity for them there.'

'With your money you can give t'bairns a fine life here,' argued Max.

'They can do better there, Max. The air is fresh and the days warm. What have they here other than fog, damp, greyness and smoke from a thousand chimneys?'

'You can move out into the country for fresh air.'

Kitty listened as Clara's and Joe's laughter filtered in from outside. 'I have thought a great deal about this in the last few days. I borrowed books from the library and read a lot information about the colony.'

Max sighed and moved to the doorway. 'I'll tekk the young-uns for a walk t'river.' He peered at Kitty. 'This is wrong what you doin'. You've got no one over there ter watch out for you like you do here.' After hoisting Rosie high on his shoulders, he marched out.

Kitty heard him call Clara and Joe to him. She gazed at Connie. 'I'm sorry.'

'Nay, lass, you must do what you think is right.' Her smile was more like a grimace. 'God chose not ter give me an' Max children an' it's been a bitter pill t'swallow. I know its medd me hard.' She shrugged. 'I didn't want ter befriend you, but summat that's been lyin' dead inside me came alive the day I met you. '

'Oh, Connie.'

'These last few months have been t'happiest of me life.' Connie sniffed. 'It's been a pleasure carin' for the young-uns.' Rising from her chair, she placed her teacup, one of Martha's, in the washing-up bucket and made for the door.

'You're leaving? I thought we were to play charades later?'

'Er… I've summat t'do,' Connie mumbled and walked up the cellar steps.

Throughout the entire exchange, Mary sat on her bed darning one of Martin's socks. Her pretty face was troubled, her eyes sad. 'They have no one but each other and us.'

'I'm going to find the others.' Jolting to her feet, Kitty put on her coat and gloves. She needed time to think. The Spencers' reaction deflated her. It hadn't been an easy decision to make, but a fresh start in a new country filled her with excitement.

Outside in the lane, a few neighbouring children lingered. Light snow had fallen again overnight, but it soon turned to slush from the many feet trampling over it. As it was Sunday, the city's streets were unusually quiet. Heavy clouds overhead threatened more snow and wisely, most people decided to stay indoors where it was warm and dry.

Kitty ambled through the streets gazing at the displays in shop windows. She caught her reflection in the glass and frowned. She didn't look old, but some days, like today, she felt ancient. Guilt at the hurt she caused the Spencers plagued her. Sometimes, it was too hard being an adult. She realized just how simple her former life had been, where the only decisions she had to make were what clothes to wear each day and what her entertainment would be. She wasn't equipped to deal with serious issues. Her governess hadn't taught her how to cope with being homeless, penniless or how to secure her family's future.

Kitty turned and stepped off the curb to cross the street.

'Get out of the way!' With quick reflexes, the carriage driver wrenched the reins and hauled his horses to a slithering halt, just inches from her. The whites of the horses' eyes glared, and snorts of steam from their nostrils jetted into the chilled air.

The driver jumped down from his seat and ran to grab hold of the nearest horse's bridle. 'You all right, miss?'

She nodded, stunned.

The carriage door opened. The driver spun to speak to the man who stepped down onto the road. 'Everything is fine, sir. A near miss it was, but the young lady is all right. Aren't you, miss?'

Kitty stared into the beautiful blue eyes of Mr Kingsley. She put her hands to her cheeks and felt them grow hot even through her gloves. 'It...it was my fault entirely. I...I wasn't...I didn't see...' She gulped. 'I...I wasn't thinking straight.'

He took her elbow. 'Are you certain you're all right, Miss McKenzie?'

'You remembered my name.' Kitty blushed deeper for sounding like a fool. *What is the matter with me?*

He smiled. 'Yes, I remember your name.'

She gazed at him for some moments before Kingsley steered her towards the carriage. 'I also remember where you live and I think you should be taken home for a nip of brandy or something. You're trembling.'

Kingsley spoke with the assurance of the gentry and Kitty was in no state to argue her independence at that moment, but she wanted to laugh at his mention of brandy, as if she'd have such a thing! She allowed him to guide her to the carriage and once seated, he gently tucked a blanket around her. He took a great liberty again, but she said nothing because being so close to him made it impossible for speech. She didn't think she could continue being near him if it meant this wild beating of her heart. Surely it wasn't normal?

In the short journey back to the lane, she wrangled with her new emotions. His presence disturbed her senses. From where he sat opposite, his long legs nearly touched hers. Her skin tingled at his closeness. Kingsley's smiling glances made her catch her breath. Although he didn't speak, she flattered herself in thinking he was taking an interest in her. She glanced at her dress and in dismay, observed it had a small stain on it. Mortified, she covered it with her hands and hoped he hadn't noticed.

Outside the cellar's little window, Kingsley helped her from the carriage. She expected him to leave her, but he walked with her down to the door. His chivalry made her tingle with pleasure.

Mary jumped up as they entered. 'Oh, good afternoon, Mr Kingsley.' She looked to Kitty for explanation.

'It is nice to meet you again, Miss Mary. Your sister suffered a mishap and I brought her home.'

Mary glanced from him to Kitty and back. 'Will you stay for a cup of tea, sir?'

'Yes, yes I will, thank you.' Kingsley sat at the table, tucking in his legs so as not to trip Mary as she went back and forth from the fire to the table. 'Are you feeling better, Miss McKenzie?'

'I am, thank you.' His company thrilled and unnerved her. His cornflower-blue eyes took in everything and she stifled the desire to tidy her hair. She glimpsed him from under her lashes as he smiled at Mary when she gave him his teacup. His strong jaw and straight nose seemed carved straight from some statue of a Greek god. Her heart thumped uncomfortably and her mouth went dry.

Mesmerized, she watched Kingsley move his long, slim fingers to add sugar to his cup and then stirred it with a teaspoon. He raised the cup to his well-shaped mouth and sipped. Over the rim, he stared back at her. Kitty blushed furiously and glanced away.

From the table, he picked up one of the books about the early exploration of Australia. 'Are you reading this?' He opened the book.

'Yes. I'm gathering as much information about the country as I can.'

'Are you?' He seemed bemused.

'Yes, we are considering moving there.'

His eyes widened. 'An interesting coincidence. I am too. I plan to leave next month to spend a year or so there.'

Her stomach flipped. She lowered her head to hide her delight. 'I'm planning to emigrate. My family and I wish to build a new life there. Have you been before?'

'No, I haven't. But my father has and he desires me to start an import and export business there. He says it is an exciting place, although very hot in the summer.'

They talked for over an hour about their plans and what they wished to achieve for the future. She sat enraptured as he spoke, watching his expressions and mannerisms, while Mary supplied them with more tea.

The arrival of the children and Max interrupted their conversation. Instantly, their rapport was gone, replaced by rushing children full of stories of what they'd seen. Kitty calmed them down, reminding them of their manners. She also introduced Kingsley to Max and the two men shook hands. Kingsley didn't play the high and mighty gentleman, pleasing Kitty immensely. It was becoming clear to her Benjamin Kingsley was no ordinary man and she liked that very much.

* * * *

'I hate this chore,' Mary mumbled, scrubbing the clothes with soap. 'I know it's hard,' Kitty soothed, ignoring the sight of her own red, rough hands.

'Can we not pay someone to do it?'

'No. The money is needed for more important things. We're capable of washing clothes.'

Mary straightened her back and looked at her. 'Are you sure going to Australia is the right thing to do?'

Kitty stopped squeezing water out of one of Clara's dresses. 'You don't agree?'

Mary shrugged. 'I'll go wherever you go, you know that.'

'But you don't want to go to Australia?'

'I…I just want you to be really sure that is all.'

'I think it'll give us more opportunities to do well, more than York has to offer.'

'But you don't know that for certain.' Mary dunked the clothes back into the water. 'Australia is so far away.'

A knock at the door halted their discussion. Kitty opened it, revealing Mr Kingsley's carriage driver standing on the steps. Her stomach flipped at the thought of seeing Kingsley again. She looked beyond the driver for a glimpse of him.

'Good morning to you, Miss I have a note here for you from Mr Kingsley.' He passed her the folded paper. 'I'll wait for your answer outside, Miss.'

Closing the door with her elbow, Kitty opened the note.

Dear Miss McKenzie,

On investigation of the library at my family home, I have discovered a small amount of books containing information about the colony of Australia. I believe they may be of use to you. I gladly make the offer for you to peruse them.

I therefore extend an invitation for you to visit my home at your convenience.

Please advise my driver as to a time and day. He will be at your disposal.

Your humble servant, Benjamin Kingsley.

'What does the note say?' Mary came to Kitty's side.

'It is an invitation to Mr Kingsley's home.'

'Oh, how exciting! When are you to go?'

Sharp disillusionment pierced her heart. 'I'm not.'

'Why?' Mary frowned.

'Because the invitation is for the use of his family's library that is all. There is no mention of Mr Kingsley even being there. He said I can go at my convenience and his driver will transport me. I've no wish to visit his library.'

She bit her lip, trying to deny the mixed feelings the note produced. It scared her to think she wanted more than just books from Kingsley.

What good would that achieve?

His offer of books only showed his generous spirit, but it also told her that he didn't want to improve on their acquaintance. Dejection welled up inside her.

'It was nice of him.' Mary smiled, going back to the washing.

'Yes…'

Mary paused. 'What is it? You don't think it charitable?'

'Of course, but…'

Frowning, Mary walked back to her. 'But what?'

'Nothing, I was being silly.' She tossed her head, hating the feeling of rejection. It was ridiculous to make an issue of it, but she couldn't stop wishing the invitation had been more personal.

Mary's eyes widened. 'You expected a different type of invitation, didn't you?'

'What is wrong with that?' She huffed. 'Anyway, it does not matter. Mr Kingsley has made it plain that the invitation is for books only.' After placing the note on the table, Kitty went to find the driver.

He was wiping the carriage over with a polishing rag. 'Yes, Miss?'

She swallowed her disappointment and summoned a smile. 'Could you convey to Mr Kingsley that I thank him for his offer, but regretfully I decline it.' She returned indoors to her washing.

* * * *

An hour later, Benjamin strode to the stables. His carriage driver, Jenkins, rubbed down one of the many horses stabled at Kingsley Manor. 'Did you deliver my note, Jenkins?'

'Yes sir, I did. I came looking for you but Mrs Kingsley said you weren't to be disturbed.'

'Was there a reply?'

'Yes, sir. The young miss said thank you for your invitation but she wouldn't be accepting.'

Benjamin tapped his fingernails on the stable door. 'Are you sure she said exactly that?'

'Yes, sir.'

Disappointed, he mumbled his thanks and turned away. 'Er…sir?'

Benjamin paused. 'Yes?'

'The young lass seemed a little upset when she gave me her message.'

Benjamin's frown deepened. Walking back to the house, he wondered what could've upset her. Was she ill? Her siblings injured? Should he go there and inquire? He shook his head and swore. No, he couldn't just turn up for no reason.

He kicked at the pebbled path leading from the stables. There was something about Kitty McKenzie that kept him awake at night. Her enchanting green eyes and copper hair made him ache with need. She intrigued him until he could think of nothing else. Despite her living arrangements, he knew she was of a quality much superior to the young women his mother presented and paraded in front him. Half of them were too stupid to know what day it was and the other half would eat him alive. He'd jumped at the chance to go to the other side of the world as a respite from his mother and Miss McKenzie's similar plans had only increased his enthusiasm.

He chewed his thumbnail. His invitation had failed. Why? Her refusal astounded him. Did she want nothing more to do with him? Had he imagined that she enjoyed his company?

Did I imagine she felt the same stirrings as me?

* * * *

Kitty sat by the fire sewing a tear in one of Joe's shirts while Rose played at her feet. The door opened and a cold draught blew in as Connie and Mary entered.

'My god, it's freezin' out there. I ain't goin' out again today,' Connie grumbled, taking off her coat. 'Ruddy snow. I'm sick of it.'

'Did Joe and Clara get to school all right?' Kitty asked.

'Aye, they did.' Connie shook the kettle to see if there was enough water in it for a brew.

Mary put her packages on the table and held her hands out to the fire. 'The shopkeepers say some of the roads out of town are completely impassable.'

'Talkin' of shopkeepers,' nodded Connie, 'I were talkin' t'old Mr Lawson an' he said he's given notice on his shop. 'Tis a shame when likes of him close down.' From a small paper bag, she gave Rosie a piece of Harrogate Toffee.

'Is that the cobbler's in Petergate?' Kitty held Joe's shirt up in front of her so she could examine her work.

'Aye. He said he's off t'New Zealand t'live with his son now he's lost his Shirley. She died two months ago. He said his son is all he has left. So, he's off next week. Seems as though everyone is off t'other side of the world.' Connie raised her eyebrows at Kitty.

Kitty's hands lay idle as last night's conversation with Martin came to mind. He told her he wouldn't go with her to Australia. Instead, he preferred to stay with the Spencers. She spent most of the night arguing with him to change his mind but he refused. He said he enjoyed his job, such as it was, and soon there might be a chance of becoming a hired hand on the boats traveling up and down the country. Martin thought it awful to leave Connie and Max after all they had done for the family.

It played heavily on her mind that her family was splitting up again. She had taken it for granted Martin would accompany them. It'd be easier to travel and set up a new home having a young man with them. Could she still do it without him? She was strong and wasn't a fool, but was she making the right decision? Could she leave Martin and the Spencers behind? Maybe she ought to make a better life here in York? And what of Rory? He might come looking for them. The thoughts whirled around in her head. The colony would be a wonderful opportunity to begin again but at what cost?

'Kitty!' Mary stood in front of her. 'Kitty, I have asked you twice if you wanted something to drink.'

'Oh, sorry. Yes, yes I would, thank you.' Rising, she put away Joe's shirt.

'You know if I had money I'd open a shop,' Connie said, wiping Rosie's sticky face with a damp towel and promptly giving the child a pear drop boiled sweet.

'What kind of shop?' Mary asked, scooping tea leaves into the teapot. 'Oh, I don't know really.' Connie chuckled. 'Perhaps a sweets shop?'

Slowly, Kitty turned to her, tilting her head in consideration.

Long after the others had gone to sleep, Kitty sat staring into the fire.

Martin crept over to sit beside her. His handsome young face wore a worried frown.

'Are you all right?' she asked softly.

'I'm sorry if I've let you down.'

'No, you haven't. I was surprised that is all. I think I count on you too much.' She smiled at him.

'I don't mind you needing me, not at all. I just feel going to Australia is not the answer. I wish you'd change your mind for I'll miss you all dreadfully.'

Kitty sighed and patted his knee. 'I'm not at all sure going to Australia is the right thing to do either, but I feel the need to do something, something worthwhile. Sitting around darning socks all day and keeping house is not my idea of living, nor is working in some grotty factory. I thought starting a new life in a new country with new people would be a…challenge.'

Martin grimaced. 'Maybe we're not as brave as you?'

'Nonsense!'

'You can do something here in York without having to go away. I know the money must be spent wisely, but for a start, we can move out of this cellar. We could easily afford to live in better rooms. That would make everyone happy.'

'Yes, true. Only, I would still be just a housekeeper and carer. I'm ashamed of myself for wanting more.'

'We all want more, Kitty.' He shrugged. 'I want my own boat. I doubt I ever will, but dreams don't hurt.'

'A boat?'

'I like being on the water.'

For the first time she saw him, not as her little brother but as a fine young man. 'When did you become so wise?'

He grinned.

'I couldn't have wished for a better brother.'

Martin hugged her. 'I feel the same way about you.'

Shortly, he went back to bed, leaving her staring into the fire. The pressure to not go to the other side of the world was mounting up. She wasn't immune to the sense of loss they'd all feel leaving the Spencers, Martin and Rory behind. Could she do it? Could she really sail away from them and not see them again for years? Was she strong enough?

Chapter Eight

The breeze whipped stray pieces of paper against Kitty's skirts as she strolled along Petergate trying to make a decision to suit everyone. To go to Australia would be an experience and an adventure. However, once there, they would be alone; just two young women and three children. The idea petrified her but she refused to live an uneventful life merely because she was frightened of taking a gamble. Many women did it, why couldn't she? She wasn't a radical or wished to incite a nation like Lady Hester Stanhope. She simply wanted her life to be accountable. When an old woman, she wanted to say she had accomplished something worthwhile.

She paused in front of Lawson's cobbler shop and peered through the window. Mr Lawson took down some shelves with a hammer. Beside him stood a short, tubby, well-dressed man gesturing wildly. Their raised voices could be heard through the glass.

As Mr Lawson turned around to take another shelf off the wall, he noticed her. Before she could walk away, he opened the door and stepped outside.

'Are you after shoes? The ones not picked up yet are out the back. Go down the side lane and up the cut at the back of the shops. There's a small gate, come in through there and pick out what's yours in the crates,' he said in one breath, not giving her the chance to answer his first question.

The other man burst out of the door. 'Listen, Lawson, I'm a reasonable man. I'm only asking that you be prepared to meet me half way on this. It's not my fault the other people backed out at the last minute! They told me they'd be taking over the shop this week. Now, due to unforeseen circumstances, I'm left short. And by rights you are still occupying the premises.' His large stomach protruded out of his great coat, dominating his small frame. He whipped a handkerchief out of his waistcoat pocket and dabbed his red face.

'Now you listen to me, Broadbent. I gave you notice as of two weeks ago and I paid in full. You've got no come back with me.' Mr Lawson stood a foot taller than Broadbent. 'It's not my fault you haven't got anyone to go straight into the shop. Maybe if you spent more time on your businesses instead of at the card tables you'd do a lot better.'

Kitty acted on impulse. 'How much is the rent?'

Both men turned to stare at her.

* * * *

The full moon shone through the thin lace curtains of the Spencer's bedroom window. Max and Connie lay in bed awake even though it was close to midnight. Since Kitty's announcement to emigrate to Australia, their relationship had changed. They ceased the evening visits to the cellar for tea by the fireside. Connie stopped going there so much during the day. As if by mutual consent they decided to wean themselves from the McKenzie family.

'You awake?' Max whispered, shifting his large body slightly. The blankets rippled in the moonlight washing over them.

'Aye. You'll be gettin' up soon, so get t'sleep an' keep still.'

'I can't sleep when I know you're upset.'

'I'm all right.'

'No, you're not an' either am I.' Propping up on his elbow, Max leaned over her.

Connie sat up against the bed frame. 'I'll miss them, Max. I can't pretend I won't.'

'Aye, lass. I'll miss them too.'

'Can't we go with them too?' she pleaded.

Max shook his head in desperation. 'Now, lass, we've been through this before. We're too old t'be traipsin' around t'other side of t'world.'

'We're not that old,' declared Connie with a huff. 'We could do it, an' we'd all be together.'

'And what do you suppose I'm goin' to do out there? I'd have no job an' we'd be dependent on young Kitty.'

Connie slipped out of bed, throwing her shawl around her shoulders. 'I reckon there'd be more jobs out there than what's 'ere.'

'But I've already got a good job 'ere. Besides, for every job goin' beggin' out there, there would be a dozen or so young fellers lined up before me. I'll not give up me job or this home for nowt! Why half of Ireland went there an' America after the famine. People won't be pullin' me off the streets sayin', *'Here have this job, mate.'* Think about it, woman.'

'Be quiet, you great lump!' Connie walked to the window and moved the curtains aside. The yard below, like all the others in the tenements, had a privy closet and a clothesline. Rubbish and waste took up the rest of the room. The smell it gave off in summer made the tenants gasp for breath. All the yards converged onto a big square where the worst of the rubbish and sewer piled. The bigwigs who ran the city promised it all would be taken away, but it never was. What the rats and feral animals didn't eat was left to pile up and rot away. It was better in the winter when the snow disguised it for a while. Soon enough though, the sun in summer would render it a steaming, stinking pile of filth again.

Inside Connie a storm of emotion swelled, begging for release. For thirty-seven years she had looked out of this window. She had spent her whole life in this house, closed her dead parents' eyes in this room. She spent the first night of her wedded life here as well. With the greatest of pain, she bled away a number of miscarriages under this very roof. She'd had enough. 'I hate that yard. I hate this room. An' if we don't go with t'others then I'll end up hatin' you,' she whispered into the hushed silence of the room.

'Connie!'

Within seconds, Connie threw herself onto his huge form and hugged him tightly. 'I'm sorry. I'm sorry. I didn't mean it, I love you, you know that.'

He stroked her hair. 'I'd do owt for you, but going ter Australia is asking too much. I'm sorry.'

'I know and I've been a stupid woman for loving them so much, for pretending those kiddies were mine.' She sobbed against his chest, finally releasing the pain and sorrow of enduring too much of a hard life.

* * * *

'A shop…' Connie gawped at Kitty. 'What about goin' t'Australia?'

'I have decided against it. I do not want to leave Martin behind or you and Max or…Rory.' Kitty sighed. 'Mary was not too keen about the idea of going either.'

Connie smiled sadly at her. 'I know what this has cost you, lass.' Taking a breath of obvious relief, Connie pulled her close and hugged her tight. 'I'm so very glad, lass. An'…I thank you for thinkin' of us.'

Kitty returned the affection, before stepping back grinning. 'So, are you going to help with this shop then or what?'

Connie laughed. 'Aye, of course.' She gathered Rosie to her. 'Just wait 'til Max hears.'

The hackney Kitty sent for waited in the lane. Very soon they alighted in front of Lawson's old cobbler shop. She had received the keys to the shop the previous day to inspect it before signing the necessary papers at Broadbent's office. The children chattered excitedly as Kitty opened the door, but for her it was bittersweet. She had given up her wishes for her family. This new venture of being a shopkeeper was intended to secure them a better life. She only hoped she'd made the right decision.

They stood for a minute looking about. The main room was one big square with a long, wide wooden bench running across the back of the shop.

Connie walked around. 'It's big enough, lass.'

Kitty stepped to the end of the bench. 'Come through here. It leads out into the backroom, which is a good size too.'

They followed her, pausing as she pointed out two small storage rooms on the left. The backroom ran the width of the shop. A narrow wooden staircase at the far end went to the rooms above. A stone sink and water pump sat beneath the window that looked out over the small courtyard outside.

'There's nowt much here.' Connie peeked out the back door. 'Looks like the courtyard is a private one, which is what you want.'

'Come look upstairs,' urged Kitty.

They took the steep, narrow staircase single file. At the top of the stairs, they stood on a small landing. A window looked out over the courtyard and a linen closet went along one wall. Only one door led off the landing. Opening it, Kitty took them into an adequately sized room.

The kitchen area occupied the wall to the left. On the right two doors opened into small bedrooms. Both rooms were the same size and shape and each had wide windows giving a view over the busy street below.

'Well, it's gettin' on in years an' could do with a lick of paint, but I like it.' Connie nodded.

'Yes, I like it to. Of course, there is work to be done. I should say a lot of work, but we'll be able to do that.' She yearned for this shop to be a success for it was to replace her dream of traveling and adventure.

'What are you going to sell?' Mary asked.

'Clothes?' Connie ran her hand over the walls to check for damp. 'You did well with Martha's stall.'

'A tea shop,' Kitty announced. 'I want it to become famous throughout York.'

'Then it'll be a toff's tea shop.' Connie sniffed.

Kitty linked her arm through Connie's. 'Yes, it will, because they are the ones who have the money to spend on having tea out. The working class are wise and have their cups of tea at home where it doesn't cost them so much. I'd go broke in a month if I catered only to them.'

'Aye, I suppose you've got a point.'

Out in the street once more, Kitty locked the door and stood back looking at the front of the shop. Above the enormous shop window was a small sign proclaiming, 'Lawson's Cobblers'. In her mind's eye, she saw a large sign above the window announcing, 'McKenzie's Tearoom'. She smiled.

She caught sight of the shop next door. It was much smaller and in a worse state of repair than the other shops in the street. Neglect showed in the peeling paintwork; a crack ran the length of its large window. The rooms above the old shop had two small windows and again one of the panes of glass was broken. Suddenly, Kitty had an idea.

'Right we'll be off home then,' Connie said, bending down to pick up a tired Rosie. 'Are you sure you'll be right goin' ter see this Broadbent fellow?'

'Yes, I'll be back shortly.'

The group parted and Kitty strode to Nessgate. Presently, she ascended a staircase between two shops, to Broadbent's offices above.

A clerk sprang to attention on seeing her enter the office. With a nervous bow, he asked her business.

'Miss McKenzie, here to see Mr Broadbent. I do have an appointment.'

'Yes, of course. Please be seated, Miss McKenzie. I'll inquire if Mr Broadbent is ready to see you.' The clerk bowed again and disappeared through a doorway behind his desk. He returned quickly to show her into another office.

Nigel Broadbent sat well back from his desk, obviously to give room to his enormous stomach.

Although it was not a warm day, sweat beaded on his baldhead and ran down inside his stiffly starched collar. He rose upon Kitty entering his tiny domain and waved her to a chair on the other side of his desk.

She sat straight and arranged the skirts of her black mourning dress. For what she had in mind she needed to show him she wasn't a simple young woman out of her depth. Raising her chin, she remembered how her mother used to look when displeased with the servants and she arranged her expression likewise.

Shuffling sheets of paper, he could only just reach on his desk, he smirked. 'So, Miss McKenzie, how did you find my property?'

Kitty raised an eyebrow. 'In need of a great deal of repair, actually.'

'Indeed? I can assure you the shop is highly sought after. I have clients—'

'Mr Broadbent. I came here today to make a business deal with you. Do you wish to do the same?' She wasn't going to let Broadbent have the upper hand.

Broadbent pulled at his collar. 'It seems I may have been a little hasty…er…yesterday.'

'Oh? The shop and rooms above aren't for rent any longer?' Kitty hid her disappointment well.

'No, I mean yes. Yes, they are. However, I believe I misled you on the sum of rent.' He took out a handkerchief and patted his baldness. 'I'm afraid it is higher than I first mentioned.'

His stale body odour was quite overpowering in the confined space of the office.

She gripped her reticule and summoned a haughty glare. 'I believe we shook hands on the amount you specified, Mr Broadbent. I always thought a gentleman's handshake was his bond?' Kitty's chin rose higher. Her childhood training in becoming a lady gave her the poise and superior manner to render Broadbent speechless. Her mother would've been proud.

'Er...um yes, of course. It's something I might have to investigate once more... The rent I mean.' He pulled at his collar again.

'I think, Mr Broadbent, we are wasting each other's time. There are other premises for rent in York. I shall make inquiries into those. Good day to you.' Kitty rose from her chair.

'No, wait! Please be seated, Miss McKenzie.' His face turned scarlet. 'I'm certain we can come to some kind of agreement.'

'If you insist on treating me as a fool, sir, then you and I are finished here.'

He began to sweat more profusely. 'No, I assure you I'm not. Please be seated and we'll start again.'

An hour later, Kitty left the building with a spring in her step. Striding down busy Nessgate, she put her hand over her mouth to stifle her laughter. What a dimwit Broadbent was. She now held the title deeds to not only the cobbler's shop, but also to the smaller rundown shop beside it. She had, in the end, not rented them but bought them lock, stock and barrel from the silly fat man. She'd gleaned from his slips in conversation that he needed ready cash, no doubt for the gambling debts Mr Lawson had hinted at and with a confidence she didn't know she possessed, she'd wrangled him down until he was begging for mercy. This new ruthless streak surprised her. She never knew she had it.

'Miss McKenzie.' Benjamin Kingsley walked along the other side of the street.

She stopped and waited while he crossed the street before greeting him. She fiddled with her sleeves while inside her stomach twisted. 'It is nice to see you again, Mr Kingsley.'

'I've been hoping to call on you. I wanted to bring you those books on Australia.'

Kitty's smile faded a little. 'I shan't be needing them now, thank you all the same.'

He frowned. 'May I ask why?'

Her heart thumped rapidly against her ribs at his nearness. 'I'm not going to the colony anymore. I have decided to stay in York.'

'But you were so keen.' Kingsley's eyes widened in surprise. 'I hoped we could sail there together.'

'I believe I'm making the right choice.' She wished she sounded more convincing. Seeing him again set her body into meltdown. 'I have to think of my family first.'

'What about what you want?'

'Maybe my time to do as I want will come later.'

They stood for a moment looking at each other. His eyes sent messages his mouth didn't utter. Kitty found words dried in her throat. She backed away. 'I must be going,'

'Now I know why you didn't use my library.'

She forced a smile. 'No doubt others will find it useful.'

'I'd like to see you again, if you wish it too.' He took her hand and bowed over it. His gaze never left hers.

Inside, her bones went to mush. 'I…I would like it very much.'

'Maybe I could take you home? My carriage is only around the corner.'

She swallowed. 'That would be lovely, thank you.'

* * * *

'You're a jammy sod,' Connie cried at Kitty. 'I don't know how you do it.'

Benjamin Kingsley had just left after spending nearly two hours with the women in the cellar. They enjoyed listening to his childhood stories. He kept them amused with tales of tricks he played on his tutor and nanny.

Kitty revelled in every second of his presence. She was drawn to him in a way that excited and frightened her. He'd listened intently to her plans for the shops, making her feel as if he hung on her every word.

'Whatever do you mean?' Kitty took on an innocent expression. 'Well, for a start you had money left ter you. Then you manage ter sweet-talk that horrid Broadbent fellow into sellin' you those shops for next ter nowt. Now, you gotta nice gentleman over the moon about you.'

'Over the moon? What tosh! Mr Kingsley and I are just friends.' In truth, she hoped Connie was right. She did want Benjamin Kingsley to have feelings for her, because she was rapidly falling for him. If what she felt was love or adoration, then she was happy to feel it for a very long time.

'Huh! Friends indeed.' Connie smiled. 'I've seen the way you both look at each other when t'other's not lookin'.'

Kitty went to the potato sack leaning in the corner by the fireplace and piled potatoes on the table. 'Don't joke about it.'

Connie leaned over to pick up a knife and a potato. 'Have you fallin' for him?'

'Yes, I think I have. Only, I don't really know what falling in love feels like so I cannot be certain.' Kitty shrugged, filling a large pan with water from the bucket. 'I'm rather scared about how I do feel. It is all so…new to me.'

'It's nowt' t'be afraid of, lass.'

'I know, but meeting someone was the last thing I thought would happen to me at the moment.'

'He may ask you t'marry him an' go t'Australia with him.'

'I doubt that will happen.'

'Owt is possible. Unless he thinks you could be his mistress, as Martha was to his grandfather?'

All warmth drained from Kitty's face. 'No, he wouldn't think that would he?'

Connie scowled. 'As I said owt is possible, lass.'

'I couldn't…' She blushed as the image of kissing Benjamin Kingsley filtered through her mind and, in answer, her body sprang to life with urges that were becoming all the more frequent.

Connie chuckled. 'Nay, never mind, I were only jokin'. I think he's smitten enough to want marriage.'

Kitty was quiet for a moment, taking in Connie's words and liking the sound of them. However, she tossed the thought away and sadly shook her head. 'If he did, I would have to refuse him. No one wishes to go to Australia, that's why I bought the shop.'

'They'd adjust, you know, an' you being married would change everythin'.' Connie nodded wisely.

'Maybe so, but I'm responsible for their happiness and, if they didn't adjust and were miserable, I would feel guilty for putting my wishes before theirs. They have endured enough with losing our parents and their old home, not to mention living in a cellar and their oldest brother disappearing, without me adding to it.'

'Aye, but—'

'No, I mustn't be selfish. It's my duty to help them become decent, happy and healthy adults. That is my priority. Besides, I doubt very much Mr Kingsley will ask me to marry him. I imagine he'd have many ladies on his list as possible brides. So, I'm not being as righteous as you might think.'

'Nonsense. 'Tis a noble thin' you doin' puttin' them afore yerself, an' that's a fact.'

'Well, noble or not, it's all I can do if I want to be able to live with myself. They are only now starting to be like their former selves. That's mainly because they have you and Max. I cannot bring myself to break their hearts by tearing them away from you both. You have replaced our parents in a way, and I couldn't make the children say goodbye to another set of parents.'

'Nay, lass, I couldn't imagine me life without you all in it.' Connie sniffed when her voice caught with emotion. She briskly peeled the potatoes.

To cover Connie's embarrassment, Kitty collected more vegetables from the sack. 'Do you think Max will agree to your living above the other shop?'

'Aye, he will. He'll do anythin' ter keep you in York.'

Kitty peeled and chopped a turnip. 'I have great plans. Knocking down the wall between the two shops greatly enlarges the area for more tables and chairs. I thought we could also do the same upstairs. That way we'd have a great big sitting room. It means us living all together as a family, instead of two separate residences. What do you think?'

'You're not just a pretty face, are you?' chuckled Connie before dodging a peeling scrap Kitty threw.

Chapter Nine

Kitty staggered with the weight of the full bucket out to the shop's courtyard. She put the bucket down for a moment to wipe her hair from her eyes and shove it back under her headscarf. Behind her, the builders' hammering echoed out into the alley.

She licked her lips and tasted dust. A glance over her clothes revealed the morning's hard toil left its mark upon them as well. Grime covered her apron and grey skirts. For a moment, guilt riddled her. She had gone into half mourning too early, but now as a member of the working class, she believed the custom could be altered somewhat to suit the situation. The upper classes might be able to afford the extra expenditure of different mourning clothes, but she couldn't.

As Kitty threw the contents of the bucket onto the stone flags, Benjamin Kingsley strolled through the gate leading from the small lane at the side. Filthy water splashed his polished, leather boots. Drops dotted his black trousers.

She stared horrified at the pooling water around his boots. 'Oh! Oh, I'm so sorry.'

He glanced down, and then at Kitty. He winked. 'So, this is how I expect to be greeted from now on, is it?' He shook each foot in turn.

'Mr Kingsley, please forgive me.'

'It's all right, really.' He grinned.

'I'm so sorry.' Kitty couldn't believe she had thrown water over the one person she wanted to impress. 'Your boots and trousers… I shall find a cloth or something.'

'Don't concern yourself over it. They will dry.' He dismissed the incident with a wave of his hand. 'I've come to see your new establishment.' His magnificent blue eyes twinkled at her.

Taking her elbow, he led her around the piles of builder's rubble and into the backroom. It was difficult for them to talk with the builder's noise, so they only stayed a minute in each room. Outside in the courtyard once more, they shook the dust from their clothes as Connie, Mary and Rosie came in through the side gate.

'Lass, we've got pasties an' bottles of ginger ale,' Connie announced before realizing they had a visitor. 'Oh, good day ter you, Mr Kingsley.'

'Good day, Mrs Spencer, Miss Mary, and how are you little scamp?' He bent to cup Rosie's cheek.

'I three soon.' Rosie held up three chubby fingers. 'What a clever girl you are.' Benjamin chuckled.

Connie sat on an overturned crate. 'Would you care for a pasty, Mr Kingsley?'

'Do you have enough?' Benjamin found another empty crate and turned it upside down.

'Aye, I bought extra.' Connie nodded to him.

They sat in silence enjoying the tasty food and letting the sun touch their faces, even though it held little warmth.

'Look at that.' Mary pointed to an early, golden-yellow daffodil growing through the pile of rubbish stacked in the corner. It was the only bright colour in the dismal yard.

'It's a grand sight ter see spring is on its way,' said Connie.

'I shall have great big tubs and fill them with flowers to place all around this yard.' Kitty took a sip of ale to wash away the dust in her throat, remembering her beloved gardens of her old home and the many hours spent walking along the flowerbeds and talking to their gardener.

'We have the most beautiful displays of flowers at the Manor.' Benjamin stretched out his legs. 'We have what we call the 'wood walk'. It's an immense grove of tall silver birches and underneath in spring there are mass displays of bluebells, snowdrops and daffodils. When a breeze blows across the flowers it looks like beautiful, colourful waves, the fragrance is quite overpowering.'

'It sounds wonderful.' Kitty smiled as he turned to her. He possessed a lovely voice, deep and rhythmic.

'Would you like to visit it one day?' His tender gaze held her spellbound.

'Yes. Yes, I would.' Joy sang through her veins. 'That would be very enjoyable. Thank you.'

After they had eaten, Connie and Mary went inside to continue cleaning. Rosie chased butterflies in the courtyard while Kitty and Benjamin stood at the gate.

'I'll come again tomorrow, if you like?' He wore no hat and a sudden cool breeze blew his fine, ebony black hair.

An immense urge to reach up and touch it consumed Kitty. 'Yes, please do come back,' she whispered, barely recognizing her voice such was the tightness in her throat. She held her hands tightly together so they wouldn't stray up to his face. Their gazes held. At any moment Kitty was sure he would kiss her. She longed for him to do that, knowing it

115

would be heavenly. It was time she experienced her first kiss and she wanted no one but him to do it.

His eyes darkened and slowly he lowered his head. Kitty sighed in anticipation, ready to feel his lips on hers.

'Catch butterfly, Kitty,' Rosie sang out to her, running up and grabbing her skirts.

The spell broke and Benjamin jerked upright. 'I'd best be going.' He cleared his throat, nodded once and left.

Kitty put her hands up to her hot face. Her heart thudded against her chest. By God! How am I going to be able to keep my feelings under control?

* * * *

Early the following Saturday morning, the whole family gathered at the shop to start the massive task of painting. During the week, the women had completed the colossal chore of sanding all of the peeling paint and washing down the walls in readiness. Doing it themselves saved a lot of money, for Kitty learned how quickly money was spent on such renovations. Her arms, shoulders and back ached as never before, but in her exhaustion, she felt proud of such achievement.

The connecting walls were down, leaving only two substantial columns as supports in the shops. A good size fireplace practically filled the end wall. It would make the shop much warmer and look homier in the winter for the customers.

'Right, Martin and Mary, you start on the walls inside the shop.' Kitty tied on her apron. 'Begin at the

116

far wall and work your way back. There is your paint over there. I have already added the colour to it. Make sure you do not get paint on the bricks around the fireplace.'

'Do you want me ter start outside?' Max asked, armed with paint, brushes and rags. A ladder already leaned against the outside of the shop.

'Yes please, Max. You know it is dark green all over. When it's dry, we'll do the two stripes above and below the sign red, and—'

'I know, I know. Yellow paint for the letterin'. You've said it a hundred times this week.' He playfully patted her on the shoulder. 'Cor! Talk about a slave driver,' he bellowed. He beckoned to Joe and Clara, who were only too happy to join the fun. 'Come on, you two scallywags. You can come an' help.'

Shaking her head at Max's antics, Kitty turned to Connie and grinned. 'Which do you want to do? Upstairs or down?'

'I'd better do down here in the backroom for I've brought food for later an' if someone don't keep an eye on it, it'll be gone if I know Joe McKenzie.' She pretended to be stern, but it didn't work and they both laughed.

Upstairs, Kitty painted the first bedroom, hers and Mary's, white. As she worked, she thought of how fulfilling the week had been. Of course, a few problems occurred. One builder fell off a ladder and broke his leg. Though the worst moment was when the building foreman gave her his bill. She found they overcharged her on just about everything. Only Mr Kingsley's intervention stopped them from robbing her blind. She did feel a little apprehensive about having used nearly all of Martha's money. The remainder would furnish the teashop. The upstairs rooms would make do with the Spencer's and cellar furniture until the shop started to make a profit.

As usual now, her thoughts turned to Benjamin. He visited every day and helped in whatever way he could. Against her wishes, he paid for all the paint as a parting gift, which showed his respect for her, but at the same time it made her read more into everything he said and did. Would a friend spend so much time and money on her? Or was he giving her hints he wanted more than just friendship? Connie believed he was in love with her, and Kitty wished she could be as confident, but what if Connie was wrong? What if Benjamin only had friendship in mind? She didn't think she could be only his friend. Every time she saw him, she wanted his sole attention, burned for his touch. It was as though he'd given her a fever and there was no cure.

Her hand stilled on a downward stroke. Paint dripped unheeded. He was leaving soon. She bowed her head. How would she bear it? At times she was angry with herself for letting her emotions get too deep. Falling in love with Benjamin had been a silly thing to do at this stage of her life. Her main focus had to be settling the children into a life without their parents and their home. She was selfish to think of herself and her needs. Hadn't the whole subject of Australia shown that? It was important that she remembered her position, and that was as a carer to her family's happiness.

'So, this is where you are hiding?' Benjamin stood in the doorway, startling her.

She blushed and was glad he couldn't read her mind. 'Mr Kingsley. How are you today?'

'Fine, Miss McKenzie and you?' He stepped into the room. 'I'm well, thank you.'

He gazed around the room. 'You look busy.'

'Yes. Watch the paint, it's still wet on the walls.' She didn't know why they were suddenly acting like strangers again, but something in his manner told her he wasn't in a joking mood. 'Is something wrong?'

No laughter lit his eyes. 'I leave on Wednesday.'

'C...can you not put it off a little longer?' Kitty put down her paintbrush. Clara's infectious giggling drifted through the open window from the street below. Everything seemed to be so normal, yet inside, his words had shattered her. Of course, she knew he was sailing soon, but to have an actual day made it all so real, so final. She stared into those magical, cornflower-blue eyes that today looked almost violet. Connie said they were wasted on a man, but Kitty disagreed. Framed by their long black lashes they simply took her breath away.

The corners of his mouth lifted ever so slightly. 'I have already put it off three weeks,' he said softly. 'I must go on Wednesday.'

Her heart seemed lodged somewhere in her throat. 'I'll miss you.'

'Not as much as I'll miss you, my lovely.'

The words 'my lovely' flooded her, washing away the disappointment and sadness of the past year, washing away any doubts she had about his feelings. She needed this affection and her reserve dissolved. She crossed the space between them, and he pulled her into his embrace. She lifted her face to his and welcomed his kiss as though it was a lifeline. He tightened his arms, lifting her off the floor. His kiss was hard, stamping his ownership on her, but she didn't care. The feel of his body beneath her hands filled her with a mind-drugging power. Their kiss deepened, his tongue swept past her lips and into her mouth. Her every bone and muscle ached with desire. Kitty pushed her fingers through his black hair and murmured against his lips.

After what seemed an age, they pulled slightly apart and grinned at each other. Kitty felt so light-headed she wondered if she would fall if he let her go. She need not have worried for Benjamin held her close.

'Forgive me?' he asked.

'Whatever for?'

'For kissing you like a passion-starved madman.'

Kitty chuckled. 'If that was a madman, then I certainly responded like a madwoman.'

He joined her laughter and kissed the tip of her nose. 'I adore you, Miss McKenzie.'

Her laughter died in her throat. 'You do?'

'Of course! You must know I love you?' Benjamin dropped a kiss on her lips.

'I…I didn't believe it to be possible.'

He held her at arm's length. 'I'm not in the habit of behaving that way with just anyone, I assure you.'

Elation sent her blood pulsating along her veins. He loved her. She wanted to cry with joy. 'I love you too. Although I have never been in love before, I'm certain this is how it feels.'

'Will you come with me to Australia? I can arrange for a special license and we can be married before we sail or even marry on the voyage.' Benjamin became infected with his own enthusiasm.

'Oh…I…' Kitty stepped away, his words shocking her. Marriage? To Benjamin? She wanted to naturally, but all within four days? What about the shop and everyone? The suddenness of it all bewildered her. Talking about it with Connie had not prepared her for him actually asking.

Benjamin frowned. 'You do want to marry me?'

'Yes, oh yes! But I cannot go to Australia now.' Happiness seeped out of her like water from a leaky bucket.

'If you are worried about the shop, don't be. I'll sort everything out and—'

'It is not just the shop. The children…'

'They can come too—'

'But they do not want to go. They wished to stay in York. It is the only home they know, which is why I bought the shop, to give them a home and provide for them. Please understand I must put them first.'

'What about us?' His face paled. 'Surely they would think differently once we were married?'

'I cannot make them leave and I cannot leave them. This shop has given them hope of a better future. They are happier than they have been since our parents died.'

'Their future would be well-taken care of with me. You will all be restored to your former positions.'

'Do you want to be shackled with five extra responsibilities?' she challenged.

'Kitty…'

She crossed the room to stare out the window. Tears blinded her. The pain in her chest tightened. She hugged herself.

Benjamin placed his hands on her shoulders and kissed the top of her head. 'I acted impulsively. Too much needs to be talked over and arranged all within four days. I realize now it would be impossible for you to make such decisions. However, I cannot delay my departure again. I'm sorry.'

'I understand completely.' But she didn't. Why does fate deal me such difficult hands?

'I'll be back within eighteen months,' he whispered into her hair. 'Would you wait for me?'

Turning in his arms, Kitty gazed up into his eyes and rested her hand against his cheek. 'I'll wait for you for ever.'

He kissed her again, pulling her into his body as though he would crush her. Sighing, he lifted his head. 'I'll make the trip as short as possible. It depends upon how quickly I can establish the businesses and make them profitable. The journey there and back alone takes months, but I promise I'll be as quick as I can.'

'I shall be here waiting, don't worry. Besides, you aren't going to get rid of me that easily.' Kitty laughed up at him.

'I never want to be rid of you, my lovely.' He kissed her softly on the lips. 'May I tell my parents about us?'

'Oh my, they don't even know I exist.'

'Yes, they do, at least they know I have been calling on you. You see, I had to tell my father why I altered the first departure date. They wish to meet you. Would tomorrow be a good time? Mother's invited you for afternoon tea.'

'She has?'

He looked guilty. 'They've noticed the change in me since meeting you. Mother suggested a visit.'

Kitty bit her bottom lip. 'Do you think they will approve of me?' 'Of course!'

* * * *

Kitty caught her breath at the magnificence of Kingsley Manor. In comparison, her old home, although large, looked like a poor cousin. When they arrived, Benjamin's parents were out visiting after Sunday morning church service. Alone, Benjamin gave her a private tour of the house. In each superbly decorated room, he stopped and kissed both her hands until it became a game and their laughter echoed throughout the house.

However, Kitty's first impression of the beautiful Georgina Kingsley chilled her. The woman wore a frozen expression of horror on her face the moment she looked at Kitty. Distressed, Kitty lowered her gaze and fumbled with her black skirts. She wore the best clothes she owned, her black skirts and cream blouse, but her crinoline was bought from the market and her black lace gloves possessed the glassy shine of frequently washed clothing.

After introductions, Benjamin's father, John, took Kitty's hand and led her into the conservatory. A maid waited by a table laden with a silver tea service and silver stands filled with dainty little cakes and sandwiches.

'So, Miss McKenzie, Ben informs us you have started a business?'

'Indeed, I have, Mr Kingsley, tearooms.' Her lips thinned into a tight smile.

They were all aware of Georgina's intake of breath.

'It is a rare thing, a young woman going into business by herself. It must have been quite a decision to make.' John Kingsley's gaze didn't waver as he looked at her.

'Upon my parents' deaths we were left with vast debts that took everything we owned to pay off. For my siblings and myself to survive, I needed to acquire a living for us all.'

Georgina put down her teacup and saucer. Her cold, blue eyes narrowed. 'Surely there are relatives who could have helped...your...er...situation?'

'I'm afraid we don't have a large quantity of relatives. No one offered to help us. There was very little we could do but sell everything.' Such intimate talk of her family unnerved her. She wished the conversation would turn to a much lighter subject.

'Did you not find that odd, your relatives turning away from you?'

'I hardly think that distant relatives, whom we rarely saw, should have to alter their lives to suit us.' Kitty hated the woman for making her defend the people who ignored her pleas for help.

'And how many are there of you, Miss McKenzie?' Georgina raised an eyebrow. She wore her disgust like a cloak.

'I'm the eldest of seven, Mrs Kingsley.'

'My, my, so many of you. So, where do you live now?' Georgina flicked an imaginary speck of dust from her beautiful, grey, raw silk dress with its crinoline so wide they had to move the chairs to accommodate it.

'We are to live above the tearooms, Mrs Kingsley.' She felt like a noose hung around her neck and with each look and question from Georgina Kingsley the knot tightened.

'How extraordinary. To live above one's own shop.' Georgina didn't hide the foul look she directed at her son.

He turned away to smile at Kitty. 'Of course, it will only be temporary, until I return from the colony. Then we shall be married.'

Georgina paled and her hand shook as she reached for her teacup and saucer. Kitty wasn't sure whether it was due to shock or anger.

John Kingsley stood and held out his arm for Kitty. 'Come, Miss McKenzie, let me show you the gardens and my fine hunters. They are the best in York I assure you.'

When John and Kitty exited the conservatory, Ben stood abruptly and faced his mother. 'How dare you,' he ground out through clenched teeth, his whole body rigid with anger.

Unperturbed, Georgina sat quietly drinking her tea. 'How dare I?' she asked with laced sarcasm. 'My dear, I don't know what is troubling you.'

'Why must you behave in such a way? She is going to be your daughter-in-law. It wouldn't have hurt too much for you to be kind to her and make her feel at ease. Instead of treating her like she was something a cat dragged in!' Ben's chest heaved.

'She is not one of us, my dear. Your union would be a most drastic mistake.' Calmly, Georgina leaned over and selected a small tart from the cake stand.

'That is where you are wrong, Mother! She is one of us. Her father was a doctor, her mother a lady. They lived well and entertained many of the people you do.'

'No, my dear. They were never one of us, for we wouldn't have let our children be thrown onto the streets upon our deaths.' Georgina contentedly nibbled her tart, secure in the knowledge of her own wisdom.

'Bankruptcy can touch anyone, Mother, even the Kingsleys.'

'Benjamin, you do realize I recall the McKenzies, especially the wife? I cannot recall her name, however.' Georgina's wave was dismissive. 'I was introduced to her some years ago at a party. And let me inform you, she was one of the most vulgar women I have yet to meet. She was loud and dreadfully flirtatious. She was attractive, I'll acknowledge that, but she was no lady.'

'I don't care a jot, Mother. It is Kitty, not her parents, who I shall be marrying.'

'Then you are a fool and you will be ruined because of it!' Georgina glared.

'Nonsense!'

Georgina took a deep breath and smoothed down her skirt. 'Darling boy, I'm only thinking of you,' she simpered. 'Your happiness is all I want.' Georgina walked over to her son and placed her hand on his arm. 'Please forgive me, my dear. I just worry so.'

Benjamin sighed. 'Understand me, Mother, please. I know you only want what is best for me, but you must realize I'm the best judge of that, not you.'

'Yes, of course dear.' She smiled up at him in all innocence.

He spun sharply on his heel and left her to go find Kitty and his father.

Georgina scowled. Was Benjamin losing his mind to bring such a person into this house? The McKenzie chit was far below what he should marry and the fact of it would have to be made obvious to him. However, she must not push him further away from her by harsh words. In a few days, he would be gone for such a long time.

Her eyes narrowed. Yes, once Benjamin was safely away, she would be able to work on that young fortune hunter. As long as she drew breath she wouldn't let them marry.

Chapter Ten

'How did it go?' Connie asked the moment Kitty walked through the doorway.

Taking off her hat, gloves and coat, Kitty's gaze travelled from one to the other. The children played on the rug in front of the fire and Max and Martin sat at the table polishing their work boots. Mary stood stirring a pot of stew.

'It went fine,' Kitty lied, hanging up her coat on the nail behind the door. After the luxury at Kingsley Manor it was hard to come back to the damp and dingy cellar.

'Were Mr Kingsley's parents nice?' Mary asked.

'Yes.' At least John Kingsley was.

'Was the house grand?' Max questioned with a smile.

Here, she could answer truthfully. 'Oh yes, the house and grounds are beautiful. The grandest I have ever seen.'

As the afternoon grew into evening, Kitty answered the children's questions until they exhausted the topic. After dinner, it started to rain. Max told the children a story by the fire until it was bedtime. When the children were asleep, Max went up to his own bed and Mary and Martin turned in also, leaving Connie and Kitty sitting at the table drinking warm cocoa.

Connie looked over the rim of her cup. 'Was it really as good as you said?'

Kitty sighed. 'You know it wasn't.'

'Which one was it? The mother or the father or both?'

'His mother.'

'Typical.'

'She did her best to make me feel uneasy. It was noticeable she didn't think I was good enough for her son. Benjamin tried to hide his embarrassment from me regarding her behaviour, but I could tell he was angry with her.' Kitty shrugged in acceptance.

'What you goin' t'do?'

She rose and rinsed her cup in a bucket of water. 'There is nothing I can do. Benjamin will be gone in a few days. I'll just have to deal with it when he returns. It is not as if Mrs Kingsley and I move in the same circles, is it?'

Kitty kept herself busy during the next few days preparing the tearooms for opening day, which was advertised to be in one week's time. She and Benjamin spent as much time with each other as possible. He organized for men from the manor to come move all their belongings to the accommodations above the shop. He accompanied her to acquire the tables and chairs needed. They bought tall, leafy green ferns and placed them throughout the tearooms to provide a little privacy for the customers. At his insistence, Ben paid for all the linen tablecloths and napkins, vases for each table, cutlery and crockery. They hunted the warehouses for display counters and curtains and spent a whole afternoon buying the ingredients needed to make the fancy cakes and sandwiches. Ben's help and support meant a great deal to her. For the first time in months, she was able to lean a little on someone else and she liked the feeling.

By Wednesday, everyone was exhausted, but thankfully, the bulk of the work was finished. Kitty sat in the backroom of the shop surrounded by boxes and crates of stock. Connie and Mary took Rosie for a walk down to the river. The others were at work and school. This left her alone to say goodbye to Ben. Her heart ached at the thought. She didn't know how she would survive the time apart from him. It was as though she'd been waiting her whole life for him to find her and to be cruelly parted so soon seemed very wrong. There were moments when she wished to ignore her duties, her family and just agree to sail away with him.

Connie had offered to take care of the children should she wish to go with Ben, but Kitty knew that wasn't the answer. She wouldn't have been happy being on the opposite side of the world from them, not knowing how they fared from day to day. And what if Rory returned? How could she blame him for deserting them when she had done the same thing? No. Staying was the only answer. Besides, eighteen months would go by quickly with them working in the tearooms, so she could wait.

When he arrived just before noon, she flung herself into his arms as he entered by the back door. Silently they held each other, savouring the moment. After a little while, she led him upstairs and they sat together on the new dark green, velvet sofa Ben had bought for her.

'How will I bear to be without you?' Kitty lifted his hands to kiss them. 'You've done so much for me, for all of us. The tearooms would never have looked so stylish without your help.'

'Money is meant to be spent, my lovely. I want to give you everything.' He kissed her nose. 'And since you'll not let me buy you a house to live in until we are married, then I must make sure this business will keep you financial until I return.'

'I feel guilty enough for all you have bought us without you keeping me.'

'What nonsense you talk, my darling. Your refusal of a bank account in your name will make me worry the entire time we are apart. However, should you find being here a struggle, go to my father. He will help you.'

'No, Ben. This is my responsibility.'

'And, as my fiancée, you are now my responsibility.'

'Fiancée?' Kitty shook her head in sadness. 'Nothing is formalized yet. Your mother—'

'It is if you accept this.' Fishing in the pocket of his great coat, Ben pulled out a black, velvet-covered box and gave it to her.

She opened the box and gasped at the beautiful emerald ring nestled on a white satin bed. 'Oh. Oh, Ben.' Tears pricked her eyes. 'It is so beautiful.'

'It matches your eyes, my darling.'

All propriety left her as she wound her arms around his neck and cried. His leaving sent splinters of pain through her heart.

'Oh, my love, do not cry. Please stop or I'll join you.' He tried to make light of it, however, his voice broke with emotion. 'Kitty, Kitty my love.'

He soothed her with soft words and long tender strokes down her back until she felt composed enough to untangle from him.

'Forgive me.' Kitty wiped away her tears with a handkerchief he gave her from his own pocket. 'It is just all too much. What about your mother? She disapproves.'

'Leave my mother to me.' He sucked in a deep breath. 'You will wear my ring? And you'll marry me when I return?'

'Yes. Oh yes.'

'Look at you.' He ran his fingers through her hair that had slipped from its combs. 'Your glorious copper hair is all awry. May I have a keepsake?'

'Of course.'

He reached over to the sewing basket resting on a side table. He selected a pair of scissors and deftly cut off a small lock of Kitty's hair. 'Do you have something I can keep this in?'

Kitty thought for a moment and then pulled out from under the collar of her dress a gold chain and locket—the last birthday gift she received from her parents.

Ben raised his eyebrows as she gave him the locket. 'Are you sure?'

'Yes. I want you to have it and for once my heart and mind agree.'

'How I love you.' Ben crushed her to him, kissing her with a thoroughness that left her breathless. She arched into him, wanting everything he gave and more. As his mouth left hers and sought the tenderness of her neck, she flung her head back, allowing him more access.

His breath, hot against her throat, sent warmth flooding through her loins. The very core of her being ached, throbbed and she shuddered in his arms.

'Lord, Kitty, I must stop…I have to stop…'

She felt his heart thumping in his chest an echo of her own beat. Kitty hid her face against his shoulder, willing her body to slow down. She breathed in his

132

particular scent of sandalwood, recalling it to memory for when she was alone. 'Write to me as often as you can.'

'I will. I promise.' He cupped her face in his hands and kissed her.

'Ben…' Every instinct in her wanted to hold on to him and never let go. He was hers and they shouldn't be parted, not now, not when she'd just found him.

'Goodbye my love, keep safe.' After one more sweet kiss, he walked away from her.

She didn't brush away the tears that ran down her cheeks and soaked into her dress. What did her appearance matter now? A sob broke from her.

Swiftly, she ran into the storeroom and rummaged through the boxes and crates until she found a calendar. Taking a small pencil out of her pocket, her fingers shaking, she crossed off today's date. She shied away from thinking how many more she would need to mark.

* * * *

'Well lass, today's the day!' Max boomed, eating breakfast at the table in their new living quarters. Shortly, he and Martin would join all the other workers trudging through the streets just after dawn on their way to various jobs.

'I'll be thinking of you,' Martin said, putting on his coat and boots. 'I hope you have a grand day.'

'Thank you, love.' Kitty handed him and Max their sandwiches and stone bottles of cold tea.

She walked downstairs with them to the backroom. After saying goodbye, she lit the fire in the range in readiness for the arrival of Alice Simpson, the pastry cook she had employed two days ago.

Nerves in her stomach made eating breakfast impossible. Kitty wandered from the range to the larder and back again, then went through to the tearooms and lit the fire in there. As the flames licked the wood, she stood and for the umpteenth time surveyed the neat tables.

Sixteen tables, eight in each room of what were once two shops. A soft cream, linen tablecloth covered each table and, in the middle, stood small empty vases waiting to be filled with fresh flowers from the market. At intervals between the tables stood the tall, green leafy indoor plants. Smaller ferns sat on pedestals. A few country scenes Ben had acquired for her hung on the newly painted walls. Snow white, lacy curtains graced the big clean windows and the swept wooden floor shone with polish.

'This is where you are.' Connie stood in the doorway, tying on her apron.

'Do you think it is too early to go to the market to buy the flowers for the tables?' Kitty placed the fireguard around the fire.

'Ye Gods lass, it's only just gone five. Come up an' have some breakfast.'

'I cannot possibly eat a thing.'

They walked through to the backroom and checked the fire in the range. At the same time, the back door opened.

'Good morning, Alice.' Kitty smiled. She liked Alice's jolly personality. The young woman wasn't a true beauty, being plump and plain. However, her cheery smile, riot of blonde curls and cooking talent outweighed anything she lacked physically. 'Please come in and take off your outdoor clothes. There's a hook behind the door.'

A week before, Kitty advertised in the local paper for a pastry cook and replies inundated her. Women of all ages applied and two days ago the back courtyard had filled with women carrying their pastry offerings. She and Connie sampled the most appalling and the most tasteful pieces of pastry in York. In the end, Alice Simpson's skills outshone the rest. Afterwards, the mere mention of pastry made Kitty feel sick.

Connie put the kettle on the hot plate to boil. 'Have you had somethin' to eat, lass?'

'Aye, a cup of tea and a couple of slices bread, Mrs Spencer.' Alice wrapped a white, starched apron around her waist and placed the mop cap over her hair. The uniforms Kitty bought weren't only for Alice, but also for everyone who worked in the kitchen and at the tables.

'Well, have another cup, lass, while you wait for the ovens to heat up.'

Connie and Alice chatted over their cups of tea until Alice decided the ovens were hot enough for her to start. With trips to the larder for ingredients, she hummed as she weighed and sifted.

Kitty and Connie returned upstairs to help Mary organize the children to wash and dress. Connie put strips of streaky bacon in a frying pan and in another pan broke six eggs. 'Lass, will you not sit down for a minute?' Connie rolled her eyes in exasperation at Kitty's pacing.

'No. I'm going down to the market for the flowers.' She pinned on her small black hat and gathered her gloves. 'Now, do you think there is anything else we need?'

'Stop worrying,' Mary said. 'You've not forgotten a thing.'

Suddenly stricken, Kitty sat at the table. 'I'm sure we'll need another person serving out front. What if we're so busy that two people out front and two out the back aren't enough?'

'Lass, you goin' to drive yerself mad. If it does get really busy, then I'll go between the two. But, until we know what's goin' to happen, let's not worry.'

Connie was right. The first day of trade disappointed Kitty. In the first two hours they only served two couples. Around eleven o'clock, five people entered, mainly gentlemen of business sitting at five different tables, which meant each table afterwards had to be stripped clean and re-laid. By two in the afternoon, they had served a total of twelve people and by closing time, at five-thirty, the amount rose to fourteen. The well- stocked display counters of Alice's beautifully made pastries and cakes as well as plates of sandwiches cut in tiny triangles mocked them.

Kitty let Alice go home at four o'clock because of the slow trade. There was no need for her to do more cooking since there was so much food left over.

Now, as the afternoon drew to a close, Connie locked the shop's front entrance and pulled the blinds down. 'Buck up lass, tomorrow could be different.' Connie put her arm around her. 'It'll tekk some time before everyone knows we're here.'

'Yes, you could be right. Though I must confess, I did hope for a better start than this.' Her day had been exhausting, mentally more than physically. Disillusionment propped up the exhaustion and Kitty wished Benjamin was there to hold her, to say all the right things she needed to hear.

Within half an hour, they had cleaned and tidied the tearooms and Mary washed up the last few dishes in the sink in the backroom.

Their jobs finished, they went upstairs and served dinner to the children just as Max and Martin came through the door.

'How did it go?' Max sat the table rubbing his stocking feet. Kitty handed him a plate of kippers. 'It could have been better.'

'Why, it'll tekk a while yet before the place is known,' Max echoed Connie's earlier sentiments.

Later, as Kitty wrote in her account books, Martin sat beside her. 'Kitty?'

'Mmm?' She didn't look up as she wrote down the day's takings and expenses.

'It's my birthday tomorrow. I'll be seventeen.'

'Yes, I know.' Kitty glanced at him, her pen poised mid-air. 'I hadn't forgotten.'

'I know you wouldn't have, it's just that now I'm seventeen, I've been offered a job on a boat. Apparently, they like my work and, well, I've made it clear to all the boatmen who dock at our wharf that I want work on the water permanently.'

'Really?' She leaned back in her chair and gave him her full attention.

'Yes, and it, the boat, leaves in the morning for Hull. Can I go?'

She blinked as if clearing her vision. When had he become a man? He worked hard for them and took his responsibility without question. He'd stepped into Rory's shoes and done a marvellous job. 'As you say, Martin, you are seventeen. You've been working as a man for some time now and I really have no say as to what road you wish to take in your life. If working on a boat is what you want to do, then you have my blessing.' Kitty bent over and kissed him on the forehead.

'Thank you. I'll still give you my pay.'

'There is no need. You save it. Put it in the bank.'

'Are you certain?'

She nodded. 'We must learn from our parents' mistakes. Money cannot be taken for granted, ever. You'll do well to remember that.'

'I will then.'

'Promise me you'll be careful and come home every time you dock in York. Is your first trip a long one?'

'I'm not sure, I only know we'll be going to Hull and from there it depends on what cargo is about.'

'When do you leave?'

'First light.'

'Well, you had better have your birthday present now then.' She smiled.

* * * *

The next morning, Kitty refused to allow her hopes to rise about the possible trade. She slept badly from the worry and hoped dark shadows didn't show under her eyes.

The first customers were two businessmen returning for a second visit.

Connie sniffed. 'It's a good sign when people come back for more.'

A surprise caller an hour after opening, made Kitty smile. The small, round figure of Mrs Halloway bustled in through the front door with an arm full of packages.

'Why, Miss McKenzie. I couldn't believe my eyes when I read about the tearooms in the paper.' She gave a Kitty a kiss on the cheek and then step back to admire the rooms. 'My, aren't you the clever one?'

Kitty grinned. 'I'm pleased to see you again. How are you, Mrs Halloway?'

'Fine, fine, my dear. I cannot stay long or my sister, Nancy, will worry, but I just thought I'd pop in to wish you luck.'

'Thank you. You're very kind and it means a lot to me. Can you not stay for some tea and cake? We could have a proper chat.'

'I'd like nothing better, my dear, but I can't today.'

Turning to Mary, Kitty asked her to box up a cake for Mrs Halloway and when Mary returned, Kitty gave it to the older woman. 'This is to say thank you for the hamper of food you gave us when we left your boarding house.'

'I don't need any thanks.' Mrs Halloway smiled, before glancing around. 'It's a credit to you, my dear. Well, goodbye, I must be off. I'll pop in again soon.' She rushed out, nearly dropping her parcels and the cake in the process.

Kitty chuckled and returned to her few customers.

Towards noon, many fashionably dressed ladies arrived. Their expensive jewellery sparkled, and their servants stood outside holding their parcels. Coming in pairs, they soon had Mary and Kitty rushed off their feet taking orders and serving. High-pitched voices and whispered undertones filled the tearooms.

Amazed at the sight, Connie peeped around the bench to gaze at them. She grasped Kitty's arm as she passed. 'Eh, lass, who'd believe it?'

'The advertisement must have worked.'

It took an hour or so before Kitty realized her lady customers took an avid interest in her. Many times, Kitty heard her name mentioned as she passed the tables. Of course, her mother's old acquaintances might have visited to see what had become of the McKenzie family, but she cared little about that. Her main concern was making the tearooms a success. If these bored ladies came to gossip, then there was nothing she could do about it. At least they spent their money in her shop.

When at last the customers dwindled down to just two couples sitting at tables by the window, Kitty left Mary waiting on them. She entered the backroom and grinned at Alice and Connie. 'Are you both still standing?' Connie flopped into a chair and fanned her face with a towel. 'Ye Gods! What got into them all arrivin' like that?' She wiped her forehead with the back of her hand.

'I thought me legs would drop off.' Alice chuckled. 'Word must've got out about me great cooking.'

'Kitty! Kitty!' Mary rushed in waving a newspaper in her hand. 'Look what was left on one of the tables.'

''Tis the day's paper, lass.' Connie poked fun at her.

Ignoring her, Mary thrust The Times into Kitty's hand. 'Look at the page it's opened at.' Mary pointed to a column.

Kitty read, her eyes widening with every word. Her and Benjamin's engagement had been announced. 'I don't understand.' The blood drained from her face. 'Who could have done this?'

'Mr Kingsley must've before he sailed,' Connie stated the obvious. 'After all, he did ask you ter marry him an' he gave you his ring ter wear.'

'But he never said he was going to announce it.' Kitty read the short announcement again. Her stomach flipped over. 'His mother will not like this.'

Kitty sent Mary up to make dinner for the children as closing time drew near. From the backroom she heard Connie and Alice talking as they cleaned. She moved a chair and swept under a table and allowed her mind to dwell on Benjamin. Why did he have to announce our engagement?

She shook her head at his logic. Did he not realize she would have to face everyone by herself? Stifling a sigh, she turned to sweep under another table when an elegant carriage and pair halted outside the shop window.

Georgina Kingsley paused on the carriage step and stared at the shop frontage. Kitty sensed the other woman's loathing. It emanated from her like an aura. Georgina waited for her groomsman to open the shop's door before regally gliding in. She surveyed her surroundings with cold blue eyes. Her gaze rested on Kitty as though it wished not to. 'I am not here on a social visit. I would not enter such an establishment as this unless it was important.'

Inside, Kitty seethed. The woman spoke as if she were visiting a brothel. Determined to be gracious, Kitty summoned a small smile. 'I'm sorry to hear that, Mrs Kingsley.'

'I am here because of the announcement published in The Times this morning.' Her disdain etched itself onto her pale face. 'You have seen it, I suppose?'

'Yes.'

'My husband and I had not been consulted. Benjamin made no mention of an engagement before he sailed.'

'I understand, but before you ask, I didn't place the advertisement.'

'My son would not have done it without speaking to me or my husband beforehand.' Georgina's upper lip curled in contempt. 'So, who does that leave?'

'No one of my acquaintance, Mrs Kingsley. I promise you.' Kitty struggled to keep check on her temper. 'Benjamin must have done it.'

Georgina stared at the ring on Kitty's left hand and her eyes narrowed into slits. 'Where did you obtain that?'

'This ring was given to me by your son, Mrs Kingsley. It is my engagement ring.' She was so thankful of the empty shop. Her embarrassment would be complete if customers saw this spectacle. She suspected Connie, Mary and Alice waited in the backroom ready to come out and help her if need be.

'That was his grandmother's ring.' Georgina's face lost its alabaster hue and grew pink. 'She willed it to him to bestow upon the woman he is to marry.'

'Then, I'll wear it with pride.'

Georgina sucked in a deep breath. 'You, miss, will not wear it at all. You will never marry my son. He deserves better than a penniless snippet like you!'

'That is enough.' Kitty put up her hand. 'I love your son and he loves me. We will be married the minute he returns from Australia and there is nothing you can do about it.'

Connie, Mary and Alice marched in to stand at her back, forming a small but angry defence.

Georgina Kingsley tilted her head majestically. Her lips thinned into an angry mark on her face. 'I can completely assure you, Miss McKenzie, that in no way will you and my son ever be joined in matrimony. If it takes every day of my life in making sure it does not happen then I'll do it. That is my pledge.'

'You cannot change Benjamin's mind or his love for me.'

'That is where you are wrong. He may be on the other side of the world, but I will make certain the letters I send him will create doubts about his association with you. He shall soon come to realize that you were just a passing interest, one that no longer requires his concentration.' She turned on her heel and strode out to her carriage. The driver whipped up the horses and it jerked into motion and out of sight.

'My God,' Connie whispered and placed her hands on Kitty's trembling shoulders. 'Aw, lass, you've got a right dragon in that one, an' no mistake. Come out back an' have a cuppa.'

Kitty sat silently while the others fussed and discussed the Kingsley woman. She longed for Benjamin's strong arms to comfort her and his tender words to confirm his love for her, but they were many miles away. She would just have to dream of them. But oh, how she missed him already and it hadn't even been a week. How would she survive eighteen months?

* * * *

Kitty waved goodbye to Joe and Clara from the gate in the side lane as they went off to school.

Already, tiredness pulled at her bones and the day had just begun. She had endured another sleepless night due to the argument with Georgina Kingsley. She was concerned that their relationship was so acrimonious. The woman would one day be her mother-in-law, yet they could barely stand the sight of one another. It worried her that Benjamin would be torn between them.

'Good morning, Miss.' A postman with a large red bag full of mail smiled at her.

'Good morning.' Kitty nodded. His uniform of waistcoat, blue frock coat with a scarlet collar, cuffs and piping were so well pressed they appeared to be new.

'Are you Miss McKenzie of McKenzie's Tearooms?'

'Yes, I am. Are you new to this round?'

'Aye, Miss. Art Tilsby is me name. Here's your mail.'

Kitty took the two letters. 'Nice to have met you, Mr Tilsby.'

'Good day to you, Miss.' The postman tipped his peaked hat.

Walking back into the courtyard, she opened the first letter. She knew it was from Benjamin and her heart soared. She paused to read the brief letter.

My Darling,
I'm writing this brief missive after boarding the ship and while waiting to sail, which will be within the hour. Although this vessel takes me away from you, I cannot help being excited by my journey.
By accepting my ring, you have made me the happiest man in the entire world. I love you so. I miss

*you already and will write again on board and post it
at my next port of call.*

*Did you see the announcement in The Times? Are
you pleased? I must go now, my love, as the last
whistle just blew for visitors to leave the ship and
with goes the mail.*

*My best wishes to all the family and again my love
to you. Benjamin.*

Kitty strolled back inside, sat at the table, and read
the short letter again.

Alice, rolling dough, glanced at her. 'Everythin'
all right, Miss Kitty?'

'Yes.' Kitty smiled at her, and then went upstairs.
She found Connie making the children's beds. 'Leave
that, Connie. I'll do it in a minute.'

'Nay, lass, many hands lighten t'load.'

'I've received a letter from Ben.'

Connie winked. 'Ben is it now?'

Kitty grinned. 'It is my name for him. His mother
calls him Benjamin.'

'Well, what's he ter say then, lass?'

'He sent it before he sailed. It was him who put the
announcement in the paper.'

Connie straightened. 'Well, we all knew that, lass.
Let's just hope he's sent a letter to his mam sayin' the
same thing.'

Kitty sighed heavily. 'I'm so disappointed she is
behaving this way. I love Ben and he loves me.
Surely that is all she should care about?'

'Aw, lass, you know better than that. You've lived
that life before. Do you think your mam would've
liked it if Rory or Martin had come home with
someone who had nowt an' lived in a cellar?'

'No, I suppose not. Knowing Mother, she would have created a fuss too. It's just I don't need the trouble it brings.'

Connie folded Clara's nightgown and placed it on her pillow. 'Aye well, just forget it for now. The dragon has some time t'get used ter it an' we've a shop ter run.'

The morning trade was slow until midday, when a few ladies called. Again, they took much interest in Kitty. Frustrated at being openly stared at, she decided to remain in the backroom as much as possible. However, she felt guilty for leaving the bulk of the work to Mary.

'Kitty. Kitty!' Mary's urgent whispering had Kitty rushing to her side and they both stared as an enormous carriage, pulled by four, proud, black horses, halted outside the shop windows. The frantic murmurings behind hands at the other tables held Kitty's attention for a moment, but it was soon diverted back to the front entrance. A small, plump, elderly lady, dressed in a coffee-coloured gown of silk with a large hat decorated in red feathers, walked in. Her hair was light grey and beautifully arranged under her hat, but it was her eyes that drew Kitty's attention for they were the most brilliant blue.

'Would you care to be seated, madam?' Kitty nearly curtsied such was the woman's regal manner.

The older woman ignored her for a moment while she took a good look around the premises. Some of the other ladies seated nodded their heads in acknowledgment, but no one spoke.

'I do believe these rooms look quite adequate,' declared the grand lady, 'and you, miss, what is your name?' She turned an inquisitive gaze to Kitty.

'Miss Katherine McKenzie, madam.'

146

'And these tearooms are yours, no doubt?'

'Indeed, they are, madam.' Kitty nodded, wishing with all her heart she had gone with Ben to Australia. She didn't know how long she could cope with such scrutiny.

'I do confess this table here will do nicely, yes?' She looked at Kitty for confirmation.

Kitty stepped forward and pulled out a chair for her. 'If madam wishes it.'

The proud little woman sat at the table by the window. She then turned to the two ladies sitting behind her. 'Mrs Pollock, and you, Mrs Seymour, is this establishment to your liking?'

Kitty closed her eyes and held her breath.

The two ladies, surprised by the question, hesitated. 'Well, yes, Mrs Cannon. We find it most agreeable,' they parroted each other.

The old woman nodded, turning back to Kitty and Mary, who hung a little behind. 'Miss McKenzie, I'm Mrs Dorothea Cannon, of Cannonvale Park. How do you do?'

'Very well, thank you, Mrs Cannon, and you?' Kitty forced a smile.

'Fine enough at the minute, though I shall die of thirst any moment.' She frowned, but Kitty saw a twinkle in her eye and managed to grin back.

'Would a pot of tea be to your liking or maybe coffee perhaps?'

'Coffee, I think. Make certain it is fresh and of good quality.' Mrs Cannon waved a hand towards the display counter. 'An array of those dainty little cakes too, if you please.'

'Of course, madam.' Kitty walked away with Mary at her heels. Going into the backroom, Kitty nearly collided with Connie and Alice who stood listening in the doorway.

'Who's she?' Connie whispered.

'A Mrs Cannon, now help me make some fresh coffee.' Kitty rushed into the larder. 'Mary, go out front and fill a small stand for Mrs Cannon.'

For half an hour Mrs Cannon drank her coffee and nibbled at the cakes Mary placed before her. It was not until the other ladies seated behind her rose, paid for their tea and left that Mrs Cannon beckoned Kitty over to her. 'Sit down, girl,' she demanded airily, with a wave of her jewelled hand to the opposite chair.

Kitty sat, not at all sure what was required of her.

'Now, let me tell you something. I came here today to have a good look at you and this establishment because of one thing,' Mrs Cannon paused, eyeing Kitty warily, 'my grandson.'

'Your grandson?'

'Indeed. You see he told me he had fallen for a young woman who was beautiful, intelligent and most of all, worthy.' Here, Mrs Cannon paused again and peered closely at Kitty. 'So, I thought I must meet this young woman to satisfy myself whether she deserves my grandson's affections.'

Kitty felt the blood leave her face. Oh, Lord. She really couldn't face another confrontation with a member of Ben's family. 'You are Benjamin's grandmother?'

Dorothea Cannon's lips twitched. 'Indeed, and I like surprising people.'

'You have certainly done that today, Mrs Cannon.'

'Let me tell you of the sensations that have come about since you appeared on the scene. My daughter has plagued me night and day over you. She has recited every detail of your two brief encounters, and let me assure you, Miss McKenzie, my daughter is a woman whom you wouldn't wish to have as a foe.'

Kitty closed her eyes momentarily. 'Please believe me, Mrs Cannon, I would be most happy to befriend Ben's mother, but alas, she will not see beyond my current status as a shop owner.'

'Do you believe you are worthy of my grandson's affections?'

'Whether I'm worthy or not is something I cannot answer. However, I do know I love your grandson most desperately and with all my heart.' Out of her pocket, she pulled Ben's letter and handed it over for Dorothea to read. Maybe then she would see the love they felt for each other.

Kitty waited while the other woman read the letter.

'Excellent. That is the first hurdle over with. It is obvious the depth of feeling between the two of you.' Dorothea returned the letter and smiled. 'Benjamin visited me before he sailed, and I was delighted at the change in him. I do accept my daughter has been at fault for Benjamin's unhappiness. She is far too controlling for her own good and I'm afraid it has all been for nothing. Ever since Benjamin was a child, all he wanted to do is be away from her and her complete devotion for him. Which in turn, distresses my daughter and makes her more determined to be closer to him.'

Dorothea sipped her coffee, staring thoughtfully out the window at the passing traffic. 'I'm ashamed that my daughter is a woman whom one cannot easily befriend. She was thoroughly spoiled by my late husband and I'm afraid John does not stand up to her as much as he should.'

'I found Mr Kingsley most agreeable. I liked him a lot.'

'Yes, dear John, he is a good man. Oh, do not have me mistaken, Miss McKenzie, I love my daughter most dearly and I love her more the less I see of her.' Dorothea chuckled at her own joke and Kitty hid a smile with her hand.

Dorothea suddenly rose from her chair and Kitty did also. 'I must be on my way now, my dear. I would like to call again, if I may?'

'Oh, yes, please do, Mrs Cannon.'

'Call me Dorothea, my dear, and I believe you are known as Kitty?'

'Yes, I am, and thank you, Dorothea. It has been such a pleasure to meet you.' Kitty held out her hand and Dorothea took it.

Together they went outside to the carriage. As Dorothea was handed up the carriage step, she paused and turned back to Kitty. 'I shall tell all my friends and acquaintances about your lovely tearooms, my dear, be assured of that. We must keep it in the family, you know.' Dorothea winked at Kitty, before resting back against the leather-bound seats. With a flick of the reins, the carriage rolled away.

Inside, Kitty helped Mary clear away the table. Securing Dorothea's friendship made her light-headed with relief. If only Ben's mother was as pleasant.

'She had lovely eyes,' Mary said, folding the tablecloth. Kitty agreed for were they not identical to Ben's?

* * * *

In the plush red dining room of Kingsley Manor, Dorothea placed her linen napkin delicately beside her plate. At the end of the dining table, her daughter sat majestically, nibbling her food. Dorothea glanced at John before squaring her shoulders. 'Earlier today, I called to make acquaintance with Benjamin's fiancée.'

Georgina choked on her food and her eyes narrowed. 'May I ask you not to mention that woman in my presence, Mother?'

'Why? She is of a decent sort and shall make Benjamin a fine wife,' persisted Dorothea. 'He loves her. Why aren't you happy that he's found a woman who will make him content?'

'I'll not have it! Do you hear?' Georgina rose quickly to her feet, dismissing a helpful servant with a toss of her head.

'Calm yourself.'

'Don't interfere, Mother. I shall not see Benjamin married to some fortune hunter who owns a teashop! Why the shame of it would kill me.'

John lowered his knife and fork. 'My dear, Dorothea is right. Benjamin needs a wife of intelligence. He would go mad within a month with anything less.'

Georgina's cold glare silenced him. 'That trollop will never be my daughter-in-law. Neither will she rule this house!'

The two serving maids glanced at each other in fear.

'You're spoilt, Georgina. You have been since the cradle. Only this time you will not get your way.' Dorothea rose also, such was her determination. 'I'll not let you ruin that boy's chance of happiness. He loves her and she loves him. I'll do all in my power to see them wed.'

'Love? She wants his money and the position of being married into a wealthy family. We would be the laughingstock of all our friends and acquaintances.' Georgina's once beautiful face twisted with spite. 'It shall never take place, Mother. I shan't let it! I'd rather him dead before married to that girl.' She stormed from the room in a rustle of silk skirts and lingering perfume.

Dorothea sat down gingerly, her bones creaking with the effort. 'She must be stopped, John. I love her, but at times I do not like her.' She shook her head and reached for her wine.

'Together, we shall make certain they marry. I'll write to Benjamin and tell him to send for Kitty.'

'It will take months for the letter to arrive and months for a reply. However, it is wiser for them to be in Australia than here, for Georgina will never give them a moment's peace.' Dorothea gazed around the beautiful room with its decadent furnishings, rare Chinese silk wallpaper and lavish tableware. She could quite clearly see Kitty as mistress of all this and knew in her heart it was where the young woman belonged, but would it actually happen? A sudden shiver tingled down her spine.

Chapter Eleven

March merged into April, and April into May. The weather grew warmer, which brought more customers into the shop as they passed by, strolling in the spring sunshine.

Dorothea Cannon, true to her word, told several acquaintances about the tearooms and these regular gentlemen and ladies kept the tearooms afloat. The spirited lady visited once a week on a Thursday, staying for an hour or so, chatting to not just Kitty, but Mary also. Sometimes, she even ventured out to the back to sit and share a word with Connie and Alice. Alice's ability at making such wonderful pastry delights interested her greatly. Dorothea confessed her own cook was far less talented.

Towards the end of May, Kitty stood filling sugar bowls at the table in the backroom. Sunshine streamed in though the open doorway. She looked up as Connie returned from delivering their weekly food orders to different stores.

Connie flopped down with a tired sigh and pointed to the courtyard. 'I think we should get some hens, our lass.'

'Where would we put them?'

'I was thinkin' Max an' Joe could pull up some of them stone flags down back end an' with a bit of wire an' some wood, they could mekk a grand hen run.'

'But why?' Kitty placed the full sugar bowls back onto a tray.

'Because Hal Dunsworth charges outrageous prices. I don't think we should do business with him anymore.'

Kitty picked up the tray and gave Connie a funny look. 'Hal Dunsworth was the only merchant who would give us an account when we first opened. The others said we would have to prove ourselves first and that they didn't give accounts out to just anyone. So, he deserves our loyalty.'

'Well, I still think it's a good idea,' protested Connie. 'I like the thought of having fresh eggs laid at our very back door.'

'If Max wants to build a hen run, he can,' Kitty relented, 'and, if you want the hens so much, you may acquire them.'

Of late, Connie worried her. Her dear friend easily grew tired towards the end of each day and wasn't as robust as usual. Putting the tray on the table, Kitty studied Connie, who sat with her eyes closed. 'Are you feeling all right?'

Connie opened her eyes and sat straighter. 'Course, I am.'

'You've been tired a lot lately. Last night you fell asleep by the fire and it was barely seven o'clock.'

'I'm gettin' old.' Connie shrugged.

'Oh, come now, you aren't yet forty! Hardly old.'

Connie stood and fiddled with a stack of napkins. 'If you must know, I've started ter go through the change.'

'The change? Are you sure?'

'Course I'm sure. I haven't had a flow for months. I was told once that you go through the change earlier

154

if you've had no babbies.' Connie nodded with a wise look.

'It might be best if you went to see a doctor.'

'Nonsense. I'll not have some bloody doctor tellin' me what I already know. 'Tis a waste of good brass.'

'But Connie, your health is more important than money—'

'No, our lass, I'll not go. So, don't be wastin' your breath. I know what's happening. I know me own body.'

'All right, if you are certain that's the problem.' Kitty picked up the tray again and entered the shop. While placing the sugar bowls on each table, she promised herself to pay closer attention to Connie. She couldn't imagine life without her.

* * * *

In the pleasant summer days of June and July, trade grew at the tearooms. The city of York basked under the blue skies and the sun's golden rays. On weekends, the city's people took the opportunity of the fine weather to rest and play. The long-awaited news of the conclusion of the American civil war raised everyone's spirits. The mill workers hoped the southern states would soon resume shipping cotton over to the numerous Yorkshire mills. People put off in the last few years might again obtain work.

In the poorer parts of town, children shrieked with laughter as they ran barefooted throughout the streets, enjoying the sun on their faces and the freedom of youth. Such world issues didn't concern them as they played their games. The elderly sat on stools smoking clay pipes while watching the youngsters and gossiping with neighbours. Huge curtains of washing hung drying between buildings in never-ending lines up and down the tenements.

The wealthy, on the other side of town, took to their open-topped carriages and gigs. Ladies strolled in beautiful gardens and picked flowers to inhale their fragrances while shading themselves with pretty pastel parasols. Summer tea parties and balls were arranged, as those who stayed in London for the winter returned to their country homes ready to socialize with friends. It was such a busy time of the year, with fox hunts and rides into the vast countryside as well as picnics, musical soirées and concerts.

Inside the tearooms on Petergate however, a sombre mood prevailed. Kitty worked liked someone possessed. She lived and breathed the teashop. She rose before first light and went to bed just before midnight. She worried about the shop, the children, Connie and Ben. She lost weight from the stress, but most of all, she lost her humour.

Kitty sat in her office pretending to work on her accounts, but her mind wandered from the neat rows of figures. If it weren't for three certain causes of anxiety, she would be happier, but the three issues worried her beyond despair.

'There you are.' Dorothea Cannon tapped her gold-topped cane on the floor in the doorway to the small office. 'You should be out in the sunshine.'

Kitty stood to greet her guest. 'How are you today?' She kissed her cheek.

'You look ill, girl.' Dorothea sat on a nearby chair. Her camel-coloured crinoline spread out like icing over a cake.

'No, not really.'

Dorothea peered at her. 'I can tell something is wrong. Can you not confide in me?'

Kitty leaned back in her chair. She shrugged one shoulder and picked at her dark grey skirt. 'I have a few worries, nothing much to bother you with.'

'Let me be the judge of that.' The older woman inclined her head and the purple feather on her hat bobbed jauntily.

'Well, I'm worried about my brother, Joe. I recently learnt he's been associating with a group of young boys of dubious character. He's been staying out late and has become rude to other members of the family. This morning, I received a letter from his school, which informed me of his many absences. So, I must deal with him and set down some ground rules for obviously I have allowed him to get away with far too much lately.'

'Little scamp,' Dorothea scoffed. 'Do you want me to have him sent into the navy? I have a retired cousin who can put him on a ship.'

'No!' Kitty put a hand up to her head in alarm. 'No, thank you, I'll talk to him.'

Dorothea sighed dramatically. 'Very well then. What else?'

'It's Connie. I think she is ill. She won't discuss it or see a doctor. Twice she has fainted this week. Alice and I nearly had heart failure when she fell. Connie believes it is the change.'

'To put your mind at rest, send for a doctor the minute she looks unwell and don't listen to her excuses.' Dorothea leaned closer to pat her arm. 'Is my grandson a worry too?'

She nodded. 'Although I can do nothing about that. Not receiving a letter in months hurts deeply. He said he would write a letter on board the ship and send it at the first port of call. If he had done this, then by now I should surely have received it. It's July. He should be there now. Have you heard from him?'

'No, and neither has John or Georgina. I'm sure he has written, but ships on the ocean are beyond our control.'

'I guess I'm too impatient.' She didn't reveal her anxiety that Georgina would do good on her threat of writing poisoned letters about her.

Dorothea stood. Her knees cracked as she did so. 'Help me, dear girl, I'm so old.'

Kitty rushed to give her aid and together they walked out to the front of the shop.

By her carriage, Dorothea paused. 'Don't lose heart, sweet Kitty McKenzie. All will be well.'

The carriage drove off, but Kitty stayed on the footpath. She bit her bottom lip as thoughts of Ben flooded her mind. He would be leading an exciting life in a new and wondrous country. She longed to be with him.

All will be well. Dorothea's words rang like a church bell in her head. But would it?

With a sigh, she returned to her tiny office. She closed her account book and put it away in the desk drawer. Four small piles of coins sat on the desktop; wages. Kitty looked at the money. She had done well enough to employ a fourteen-year-old girl, Mildred Hollings. Mildred helped in both the shop and the backroom in whatever way she could and, although she hardly spoke a word to anyone, she could work better than most twice her age.

As well as Mildred, Kitty had hired a cleaning woman. A childless widow named Hetta Smith, who came in every day to clean, wash and iron. The obvious difference between Mildred and Hetta apart from age was noise. Mildred was not only quiet but also terribly shy whereas Hetta was loud, talkative and a gossip. Yet thankfully, the cleaning lady was a kind and generous soul too.

At the sound of the back door opening, Kitty left the room.

'It's hot enough to fry an egg on the flags out there,' declared Hetta as she and Connie entered carrying groceries.

Kitty smiled at the sight of Hetta's hot cheeks and picked up a tray of scones, but Connie's pale face, by comparison, worried her.

Alice cut up a lemon and added it to a jug of cooled water. 'In summer, I like spending Sundays down by the beck.'

Connie set down her basket and picked up the jug. 'I'll tekk it through to the counter.'

A moment later, a splintering crash and then a thud shattered the quietness of the rooms.

Kitty hurried into the tearoom and found Connie lying on the floor. 'Connie!' She fell to her knees beside her stricken friend. 'Dearest, speak to me.' She looked up at Hetta. 'Tell Mary to run for a doctor!'

Kitty stroked Connie's forehead. 'Connie dear, can you hear me?' Connie slowly opened her eyes and focused on her. 'Lie still, dear, the doctor has been sent for. You'll be fine.'

'Lass… What's wrong…with me?'

'We will soon find out and have you better again.'

Later, Kitty, Mary and Alice sat for an hour around the table in the backroom while Mildred and Hetta closed up the shop. Max, hurriedly sent for, waited upstairs for the doctor to finish his examination.

Kitty stood and paced the floor, her skirts swishing loudly in the quiet of the room. Impatient to hear of any news, she longed to rush upstairs to see Connie and speak to the doctor, but she knew Max wanted time alone with the doctor first.

'I'll put the kettle on, Miss.' Alice brewed another pot of tea nobody drank.

Movement from the stairs stopped everyone as the doctor descended. Hetta and Mildred come in from cleaning the tearoom to hear.

Dread clogged Kitty's throat. 'What is the news, Doctor Myers?'

'Well, Miss McKenzie, it's not what you would expect I think.' The doctor sighed and shrugged on his coat that Mary handed him 'Mrs Spencer is with child. Nearly six months along I would say.'

'With child?' Shocked, Kitty stared at the man as though he had two heads. 'She thought she was going through the change.'

'Why she should think that is beyond me. She has tiredness, fainting and enlargement around the waist, albeit not as much as she should and that is a cause for anxiety. Indeed, there are many causes for anxiety about Mrs Spencer's confinement.' He swept his tired gaze around at the worried faces staring at him. 'She has suffered many miscarriages in the past when she was much younger. To be honest with you all, and as I have already told Mr Spencer, I doubt she will carry this baby full term. If she does, I cannot guarantee that either she or the child surviving its birth.'

There was an audible intake of breath from everyone.

'Why is that then, Doctor?' Hetta asked, folding her arms over her enormous chest in a huff, her small brown eyes peering at him. 'Our Mrs Spencer is a strong woman.'

'Her past history tells me this pregnancy is not what she should be having at this time of her life.' He picked up his bag from the floor.

'You talk as though she was in her dotage,' scorned Hetta.

'Hetta, please,' shushed Kitty.

The doctor turned to Kitty, ignoring the older woman's outburst. 'She must have complete bedrest, and with the bed-end raised at all times. Her bleeding must be controlled, or, well...you can imagine the consequences.'

'She will get the best possible care, Doctor,' Kitty put in quietly. 'Surely that, and good food, will be all she needs. Nature will take care of the rest, won't it?'

'Yes, nature will take care of the rest, Miss McKenzie, one way or another.'

Once the doctor left, Kitty climbed the staircase. This unexpected news threw her into turmoil.

Max was gently closing the bedroom door as she entered the sitting room. He enveloped Kitty in his arms. 'Oh, lass. What are we t'do? She shouldn't be havin' any young'uns. She nearly died the last time. I couldn't tekk it if somethin' happened ter her.'

'Nothing is going to happen, Max, and don't ever say anything like that again. I'll take care of her and all will be well.' Dorothea's words slipped out and Kitty swallowed her sudden tears. 'At the end of it you will be a proud father of a beautiful little baby.'

'I pray that you're right, our lass, I really do.' Max kissed her on the forehead, and then went downstairs and returned to work.

Kitty crept into Connie's bedroom to sit quietly on a chair beside the bed. Connie looked pale but rested.

Kitty took her friend's hand in her own. 'How do you feel, dearest?'

'Better.'

'Good. I'll go down and make you some tea.'

'Wait.' Connie gripped her hand as Kitty moved away.

'Did you speak ter the doctor?'

'Yes.' Kitty grinned. 'So, we are to have a baby to spoil?'

Connie grimaced. 'Don't get too excited. The doctor said me chances are slim.'

'Well, we'll prove him wrong, won't we?'

'I've been through it all before, our lass. It doesn't happen t' be nice, believe me.' Connie sniffed. 'I'm surprised I've gotten along as far as I have. Six months. 'Tis a record for me.'

'Well, that is a good omen to begin with and you're going to have the best of everything to see you through to a happy end.'

'Oh, lass.' Tears tripped over Connie's lashes and ran down her cheeks.

'No! Stop it, Connie. No tears. Save them for tears of joy when you're holding your little baby in a few months' time. We must think positively about this, I mean it.' Kitty wagged a finger at her. 'Sit still, I'll go arrange some tea and a light meal.'

* * * *

Kitty sat on a chair in the courtyard and watched Clara and Rosie feed the hens. The August heat warmed her body though her heart was as cold as ice. Joe had played truant again at school but refused to discuss the subject that morning at breakfast before disappearing for the rest of the day. She wished Mr Tilsby, the postman, would bring her good news instead of notes from the school. She ached for word of Ben, but each day nothing arrived. Doubts and frustration fought a duel in her mind whenever she thought of him. Why had she received no more letters? Had he second thoughts now he was away leading an exciting life?

'Is Mrs Cannon coming this evening?' Clara asked, dusting crumbs off her hands.

'I thought she was, but it's past her usual calling time. She may have visitors and it has slipped her mind.'

Mary ran out to them, her face white and her eyes wide. 'Kitty! Kitty!'

'What is it?' She jerked to her feet. 'Connie?'

'There is a policeman waiting to speak to you. He asked specifically for you.' Mary gasped. 'Shall I bring him through? The customers are whispering amongst themselves.'

'Yes, yes bring him into the backroom.' Kitty fished for a coin in her pocket and pulled out a penny. 'Clara, take Rosie to the sweet shop. Hold her hand and come straight back.' As soon as they stepped through the gate, Kitty straightened her hair and skirts. Taking a deep breath to still her panic, she went inside.

She nodded at Alice, who left the range and stood behind her for support. Together they faced the tall policeman who came into the backroom, removing his hat as he did so. Mary scuttled around to stand behind Kitty on her other side.

Please don't let it be Rory or Martin.

163

'Miss McKenzie?' the policeman spoke directly to Kitty.

'Yes?' She looked him in the eye, bracing herself for bad news.

'My name is Constable Mike Bentley. I've been sent to inform you that your brother, Joseph, is in our cells. He was caught stealing.'

'No.' The blood drained from her face and her knees buckled. Alice's arm slipped around Kitty's waist in an effort to keep her upright. Mary cried into a handkerchief.

'You'll need to come with me down to the station, Miss.'

He waited while Alice and Mary helped to find Kitty's reticule and coat and quickly pinned on her hat. Hardly aware of what she was doing, Kitty remembered to whisper to Mary not to let Connie know so she wouldn't worry, and then followed the constable out the back door.

Chapter Twelve

Kitty thought she had experienced fear before, the fear of not finding her brothers and sisters a home after her parents' death, the fear of not being able to feed and clothe them, the fear of living in a damp and freezing cellar. Yet nothing prepared her for the intense fear that descended on her as she walked the cold, dark, moisture-dripping stuffiness of the gaol's underground corridors. Beside her stepped the tall constable, who had to bend his head every time they went through the cramped archways of the gaol's tunnels. In front of them both, shuffled the turnkey of the cells.

The turnkey, a large fat man who stank like those who washed neither clothes nor body, led them down a winding maze of slippery tunnels until he halted and grunted towards a thick cell door. After producing an array of keys on rings from his broad belt, he opened the steel-studded, wooden door. Spluttering oil lamps secured in iron braces high up on the walls gave off a sharp rancid smell and their dim light didn't penetrate the cells.

The constable brought with him a large oil lamp, and with this held high, he entered the cell and called for Joseph McKenzie to stand and present himself.

After a moment there was a shuffle, a few groans and then Joe stood before them, dirty and humble.

Kitty lurched forward to drag him into her arms. 'Joe. Oh, Joe, are you all right?'

The constable peered at Joe. 'You acknowledge this boy is your brother, Miss McKenzie?'

Kitty nodded. 'Yes. Yes, he is. Can he come home now?' The ugly, fat turnkey chuckled.

The constable shook his head. 'I'm afraid not, Miss. He is to appear before the court and be sentenced.'

'Sentenced? But he's only a boy? Whatever he stole I'll pay back. I give you my word.'

'I'm sorry, Miss. There is nothing I can do. I suggest you find someone to represent your brother, if you can afford it. He will appear before the judge tomorrow week at the court house.'

Dizziness washed over her.

Joe snivelled as the three other youths in the small stinking cell sniggered at him. She used her handkerchief to wipe the grime from his face. 'Shush, now,' she whispered and then glared into the cell as a warning to the lurking, laughing figures hidden in there.

'Quiet,' the turnkey yelled at them. His voice echoed around the confines of the underground tunnel.

Kitty hugged Joe to her. 'Everything will be fine.'

The constable cleared his throat. 'We must leave now, Miss McKenzie.'

Joe held her tight and wouldn't let go. Kitty hated to force his arms from around her, but she kissed him and promised to be back the next day.

As they neared the end of the dim corridor, the turnkey tapped her arm, halting her. 'If you wish for you brother t'be a bit more comfortable then just pass me hand with a few bits of gold an' I can see that it

happens.' He winked at her just before the constable
turned, asking her to come along.

Outside in the fresh air, Kitty took deep breaths to
quell her nerves. The stink of the cells coated her
clothes and filled her nose.

'Did the turnkey ask for money to see your brother
right, Miss McKenzie?' Constable Bentley eyes
narrowed.

'Er… Yes, yes, he did,' mumbled Kitty, still
shocked by the sight of Joe in prison.

'My advice is, miss, don't do it. Any money you
give old turnkey Griggs will only line his own
pockets. He's not to be trusted, believe me.'

The walk back to the tearooms passed by in a daze.
Joe being in gaol made her tremble and feel sick.
How had it happened? What possessed him to steal?
Didn't she give him all he needed? The thoughts
whirled around in her head.

'Kitty. What happened?' Mary waited for her at
the back door and led her upstairs and onto the sofa.
'Where is Joe?'

'He couldn't come home, not yet.' She rubbed her
hand over her eyes. 'I hated leaving him there.'

'Why did he do it?'

'I didn't ask him why.' Kitty shook her head.

Alice brought up a tea tray. 'I've asked Mildred to
close the shop, Miss Kitty.'

'Thank you, Alice.' Kitty explained the situation
to them both and in doing so felt better. She began to
plan what she must do. She needed help, but who
could she turn to? For the umpteenth time she wished
for Ben's presence, his arms to hold her.

When Max returned from work and heard the
news, they decided to explain Joe's absence to
Connie and the younger children by saying Joe had

gone to stay at a friend's house for a few days. Clara found the explanation a little hard to fathom as all of Joe's friends had been playing near her and her friends today and she had not seen her brother. Kitty kept her occupied with little chores and eventually Clara questioned no more.

'If he's found guilty, lass, he could be sent down for a long time,' Max murmured once the children were in bed.

'Do they still transport them to Australia?' Kitty asked, the quiver remaining in her voice. She stayed away from Connie so as not to alert her sharp wit to anything wrong.

Max frowned. 'No, I don't think so, but I can't be sure.'

Kitty clenched her hands in her lap. 'They…they wouldn't hang him surely?'

Max pulled her roughly to him. 'Nay, lass! Don't think that.'

She leaned her forehead against his wide chest. 'I cannot stand it, Max. What is happening to my family?'

* * * *

Kitty dressed in a new skirt and short jacket of dark grey trimmed in black. The half-mourning clothes she wore were a fitting tribute to her despair and matched the shadows under her eyes. She left the house early, before the others awoke, and caught a passing hansom cab.

The large, impressive stone building of York Police was busy even though the sun just peeked over the rooftops. Kitty ignored the stares as she asked to see someone in charge.

The elderly sergeant's eyes regarded her solemnly from under thick, bushy eyebrows. 'Miss McKenzie, I cannot convey police information to you. Your brother is to come before the magistrate. The gentleman your brother stole from is quite adamant that he will not drop the charges. Nothing can be done by you I'm afraid, except to enlist the services of someone to represent your brother.'

Kitty leaned forward. 'If I knew the gentleman's name, I could go and see him. If I could talk to him, he may be willing to drop the charges against my brother. I must do something to help him.'

She pleaded with the sergeant for a further ten minutes before he put up his hand, drawing the conversation to a halt.

He showed Kitty out onto the street, but before she turned away, he took her elbow, whispered a man's name and address, then quickly disappeared into the building.

Clinging to the small hope she could beg for mercy with the unknown gentleman, Kitty hurried down the street and hailed another cab. The gentleman's name was familiar—perhaps an old acquaintance of her father's. She breathed a little easier knowing that one of her own kind would listen to her.

The cab deposited her in a wide, tree-lined street. Three-story houses stood in tended gardens behind low iron and stone fences. It was a street not unlike the one where she used to live. She shook the depressing thought from her mind and banged the brass knocker against the black painted door of number seven.

A butler answered the summons and, after inquiring about her business, let her enter to stand in the tiled hall. After a few minutes, he returned to usher Kitty into a small room further down the hallway.

Inside the room, Kitty glanced at the number of books lining the walls and the huge desk that dominated the room. A middle-aged man expensively dressed in a dark brown suit, with sharp eyes and a receding hairline stood with his back to the window. His haughty stare focused upon her as she stepped further into the room.

'Good morning.' Kitty smiled and hid her trembling hands behind her back.

He scowled and sat at his beautiful walnut desk. 'Miss McKenzie, I believe?'

'Yes, I am.' His patronizing gaze made her hackles rise, but she focused upon the issue at hand. He continued to glare at her as though she was beneath him and he reminded her of Georgina Kingsley. 'Please, may I say that I deeply regret my brother's intolerable behaviour and I assure you he has never done anything like this before—'

'Nor will he do so again.' The gentleman's eyes narrowed.

'Please, sir, if you could just see your way to dropping the charges against my brother—'

'Your brother needs to be taught a lesson. People of your kind cannot roam the streets committing crimes against the decent people of this or any other town.' The gentleman's voice had risen, and he visibly shook himself to check his temper while glowering at Kitty.

Shivers ran along her skin. 'B-believe me, my brother will never, ever act in such a disgraceful way again. He was not brought up to behave like that. My parents were well educated—'

'And were also thieves, but on a larger scale,' he growled between clenched teeth.

'P-pardon?' Her stomach clenched in dread of the man's angry words. This wasn't going to plan.

'Your father died owing me over two hundred pounds. A sum I was never able to recover. And now your brother continues with the family trait and steals my wallet.' The man jerked to his feet and stalked around the desk to stand in front of her. He raised a fist and shook it in the air above Kitty's head. 'I'll not be robbed again by a McKenzie.'

Mortified, she stumbled back. 'Did…did you not come to the house and reclaim something of value to compensate? Notices were sent out after my parents' death.'

The gentleman laughed cruelly. 'No, begod. I was in London at that time and only learned of it on my return. By then, it was too late.'

'I…I'm sorry.' She tried to find the courage to fight him with words, but her mind had frozen. 'Please don't punish my brother for my father's mistakes.'

'Ah! Have you forgotten that your dear little brother has also stolen?' A nerve pulsed along his left eyelid. 'Your brother will spend the next ten years of his life rotting away in some gaol or he may be sent to Botany Bay, they still do that I'm told.'

Kitty's eyes widened in horror. To be sent to Australia as a convict. She couldn't bear it.

He looked smug. 'Consider your father's debt as now being repaid.'

She stumbled from his study, his mocking words haunting her.

* * * *

Kitty sat at the kitchen table upstairs out of the way from prying eyes, unable to put on a happy face for the customers. She knew the others could organize the tearoom. Overcome with despair, Kitty stared into the fire and hoped that, when she took Connie her tea, she wouldn't ask too many questions about the tense atmosphere pervading the house.

The rustle of skirts preceded Dorothea as she glided into the sitting room. 'My dear, this will not do.'

Kitty rose to kiss her cheek. 'You received my note?'

'Indeed.'

'I'm so sorry to bother you with my troubles, but I had no one else to turn to.'

'Stuff and nonsense. We're family or soon will be. Now, tell me everything.'

When Kitty finished telling the story, Dorothea shook her head. 'A fine mettle that boy has landed himself into, but don't despair, dear girl. It will be sorted.'

'How?' Kitty paced the floor. 'That…man holds a grudge against us just to get his revenge against my father. I cannot believe we're still paying for our parents' folly. Wasn't living in a cellar enough? I have already lost one brother and cannot afford to lose another.' Kitty massaged her temples. She had to remain calm. Connie mustn't hear her and become upset.

'Come, sit down, dear.'

'I cannot bear the thought of Joe rotting away in some gaol...'

'You're becoming dramatic, my dear. Please, come sit down and listen to me.' Dorothea beckoned and waited while she took her place on the sofa. 'I was not idle yesterday after I heard the news. I went to see a lawyer friend of mine who is going to the gaol this morning. We'll have young Joseph home before you know it.' Dorothea patted Kitty's hand and smiled.

'Really? You mean Joe may be allowed home?' Relief made her light- headed.

'I'm sure of it. I have many influential friends and a few favours owed to me. Also, I have spoken to John and he will act on your behalf too.'

'This will free Joe?'

'I don't doubt it. However, Georgina is not very pleased with this latest ordeal. It's given her more excuses to argue that you're not fit to marry Benjamin. You must ensure Joe stays out of further trouble. Otherwise my daughter will delight in using him in her bid to keep you and Benjamin apart.'

'I understand.' Kitty nodded, her estimation of Georgina lowering another notch. 'I imagine Georgina took pleasure in my despair?'

'Not pleasure, no, but she did mention it as further proof that your union with Benjamin would be disastrous.' Dorothea sat straighter. 'Enough of that. We must concentrate on Joe and his release.'

'Oh, Dorothea. How can I ever repay you?'

Dorothea winked. 'Well a good start would be to make us some tea while I go and sit with Connie.'

It was after six that evening when Joe walked into the sitting room to a huge welcome. He was dirty, hungry and a little overwhelmed, but Kitty and Mary soon had him in the bath and scrubbed. In a clean nightshirt, he ate his meal of boiled beef and vegetables as though he had not eaten in months. Before long, his head drooped with fatigue.

'Come, Joe.' Kitty helped him from the table.

She saw him into bed and sat beside him, tucking the blankets up to his chin. Never in her life would she be able to repay Dorothea for bringing Joe home again. She hadn't asked questions as to how it had come about. She was just grateful for the deliverance of Joe back into her care.

Joe gazed up at her with teary eyes. 'I'm sorry, Kitty. I didn't mean to cause any trouble.'

'Well, you did. Why did you do such a thing?'

Joe shrugged. 'I suppose…to show I just could, that's all.'

'You stole because you could?' Kitty turned away, her anger throbbing, desperate for release. 'I'm ashamed of you.'

'I'm sorry.'

She spun back to him. 'Did you recognize the man?'

'No, he was flashing his money as he came out of a shop. He's just a toff!'

'Like we were?'

The colour left Joe's face. 'We aren't anymore, are we?'

'Is that why you did it, because we no longer have a nice house and money?'

He shrugged again and refused to meet her gaze.

'We'll discuss this another time, but I'm letting you know right now, Joseph McKenzie, if you ever do such a thing again, I'll let them send you to gaol. Do you understand me?'

A slow tear trickled down his cheek. 'I'll not do it again, I promise.'

'Well, you'll not be allowed the chance to do it again. As of tomorrow morning, both you and Clara are going to start at a new school. A school that is of a bit higher standard than the one you both attend now. It will cost me a lot of money, but it will be worth it if it keeps you out of trouble.'

'I don't want to go to another school, Kitty. Please don't send us somewhere else.'

'It's for the best, Joe. I'll not have you mixing with the likes of those boys you play around with. They're worse than the children from the tenements. When we left the cellar, I should have moved you and Clara to a new school closer to the tearooms. However, I thought you would prefer staying at the same school near Walmgate. I see now I was wrong.'

'But, Kitty—'

'No, Joe! No more talking. My decision is made.'

'But—'

'Do you realize how close you came to being in gaol for years?' Her tone lashed him, trying to make him aware of how close he came to ruination.

He lowered his gaze. 'Yes.'

'Well, just you think about it some more and be thankful we have wonderful friends like Dorothea Cannon. Now off to sleep, you have a big day tomorrow before and after school.'

Joe struggled to sit up as Kitty moved away. 'What do you mean?'

Kitty turned at the doorway. 'You, young man, have a full day's work ahead of you. I obviously let you have too much freedom, which you have now forfeited. So, there are many little jobs around the shop that are your responsibility from now on. You didn't think you could frighten the life out of me and get away with it, did you? Changing schools will be the least of your worries, my lad.'

* * * *

'This heat!' Hetta complained for the tenth time that morning as she stepped in from outside after emptying her bucket of dirty water. 'I wish we would get some rain.'

Mary and Kitty exchanged amused glances as she passed, before continuing to check the stock needing to be bought by the end of the week.

'Ladies, what a grand day it is,' Art Tilsby, the postman, called to them through the open back door. He handed Kitty a small pile of mail.

'Would you care for a drink of cold lemon water, Mr Tilsby?' Kitty placed the mail on the table. She hated the mail. It never brought news of Ben or Rory.

'Aye, I would that, Miss McKenzie. It's like an oven out there.' He slipped off his hat to wipe the sweat from his brow. He smiled and nodded at Mary, who poked her head out of the larder to say good morning. Alice made conversation with him while Kitty poured drinks for everyone.

He accepted his glass with a small bow. 'I always liked hot August days when I was a kid, but now I think I'm too old to deal with such heat.'

'It's unusual to be hot for so long,' acknowledged Alice. 'Three weeks of constant blazing days. I've never seen the likes of it before.'

Mr Tilsby drained his glass and placed it on the table. 'Thanks for that, it did the job grand. I best be on my way now though.' Before reaching the door, he paused to smile at Kitty. 'I nearly forgot, miss, there's a letter there all the way from Australia. Imagine the distance it's travelled?' With that parting remark, he left.

Kitty turned very slowly and picked up the mail from the table. With trembling hands, she selected the letter with Ben's familiar handwriting. Her heart felt like it would stop any moment. She grinned at Mary and Alice and then ran upstairs to the privacy of her bedroom.

Tearing open the envelope, Kitty pulled out the few sheets of paper. She held them to her face in wonderment. Her heart beat a tattoo against her ribs and her stomach churned in anticipation.

Taking a deep breath, she began to read.

Dearest darling Kitty.
My love, I cannot begin to tell you of the delights of the city. Sydney is a wonder, but first I must ask after your health and that of the family. I pray you are all well.
Kitty, you would adore it, the sense of adventure that surrounds the area. The harbour is a delight, a natural beauty and so exciting with foreign ships continually coming and going. There are people of all nations here starting new lives, but of course the British influence is prominent everywhere. There are times when you actually feel you are home in England. One can pass through crowds and hear every accent of our country in one street.
Since arriving here on the last day of May, I have been extremely busy meeting people of Father's

acquaintance. Starting our own branch of business will not be as hard as I imagined. I'm fast making many contacts and, indeed, good friends. Soon though, I'll have time to investigate this land of opportunity. I admit it excites me that I shall be venturing further than the boundaries of Sydney and into the open countryside.

I'm told expedition parties leave at regular intervals to explore the vastness of this hot dry land and new townships are simply evolving in a matter of days in places where a few weeks before there was only impenetrable bush. The exciting activity here, Kitty, makes me eager to finish my work in the city and be off delving into the bush.

I sincerely hope you are missing me and that I still have your love. I wish with all my heart you were here beside me, for I know you would love Australia as much as I have come to. There is space here to just breathe.

Did you enjoy my last letter I posted on route? Rio was a delight but terribly hot. I'll write again before the week is out. I long to hear from you. It has been a torture not knowing how you are and being unable to gaze upon your beautiful face. Don't stop writing to me. The mail is slow to reach us sadly.

Give my regards to everyone. To you, my dearest heart, I give all my love.

In my thoughts always, Benjamin.

Kitty read the letter twice again before crossing to Connie's bedroom. She tapped gently on the door and entered. The last month of resting had put weight on Connie's thin frame and she looked healthier. There were more grey hairs in amongst her own natural brown now and a few extra worry lines graced her face, but Dr Meyers, who called once a week, was happy with her progress.

Connie reclined against pillows, knitting a sock, and smiled as Kitty came in. 'How's everythin' goin'?'

'I just received a letter from Ben.' Kitty stroked it lovingly.

'Oh, lass, I'm that pleased for you. Is he all right?'

'Yes, he sounds extremely happy. He sends his regards to you all. He had sent another letter, but I haven't received it.' This saddened her for a moment, but she quickly brightened again and kissed the letter.

'Well, never mind, our lass. At least you've got this one an' that's better than nowt.'

Kitty sat on the bed. The letter had lifted a weight off her heart. She had doubted his love would continue once he had left her, but having proof released a wave of emotion. She didn't know whether to laugh or cry. 'Shall I read it to you?'

'Aye, go on then, for I'll get no peace until you do.' Connie laughed.

Chapter Thirteen

Kitty added another shovel full of coal to the fire. The late October winds battered against the windows as though seeking for way to enter. She turned and smiled at Martin, who was making one of his infrequent visits home. He had grown an inch and his shoulders had broadened. His black hair fell long over his collar and he hadn't shaved for days.

Martin placed his teacup on the table. 'I have some news.'

'Oh? Tell me you haven't met a fine young lady?' Kitty smiled and passed around a plate of small cakes not sold during the day. Her buoyant mood resulted from receiving another letter from Ben, which she had just read to the family.

'No.' He avoided Kitty's gaze and looked at Max as a blush stained his stubble-covered cheeks. 'I'm to voyage to India, then through the Pacific Islands and on to Australia.'

A heavy silence descended.

Joe swallowed a mouthful of cake. 'I wish I could go to India and see elephants.'

'Me too,' added Rosie, half asleep cuddled up on Max's lap.

Martin ignored Joe and Rosie as he continued. 'I've been offered a job on a ship that leaves in a week from Portsmouth. The owner wants to trade in the South Pacific. Sydney will be his base.'

They all stared at him.

He looked at Kitty. 'Aren't you happy for me?'

'Happy?' Kitty jumped from her seat. Anger burned inside her chest, nearly suffocating her. 'I don't believe it!' In a fit of temper, she slammed down the plate of cakes; some of them tumbled onto the table.

Martin reared back under her onslaught. 'Kitty, I—'

'I cannot believe you're leaving us to go to the one place I wanted us to go in the first instance. We all had the chance to live there with Ben. Do you realize what I gave up because I thought you all wanted to stay here, together? I'd be married to Ben by now!' As she stared at them, daring them to deny it, tears threatened to spill.

Mary reached for her hand. 'We're still together.'

Kitty spun towards her. 'Are we? Rory is God knows where and Martin is to travel to the other side of the world where Ben is. How is that being together? I let Ben go alone because you all said staying here was better.'

Martin slowly rose from his chair. 'Kitty, I'm sorry. I didn't know I would love seafaring so much.'

'You said you wanted to stay here.'

'I thought I did, but I've seen so much these last few months and I want to see more. I'm sorry.'

Max stood, placing Rosie on his chair. He faced them both. 'Let's not shout like fishwives.'

'I'll shout all I like, Max Spencer! I have earned the right,' Kitty spat.

Martin plucked at his trousers. 'I never expected to spend my life this way or to be so passionate about it. When I'm out on the open water it's the most wonderful feeling. I know I only go up and down the coast and I was happy with that, until I met Captain Peterson. He liked the fact I'd an education and he said I could go far. I could even study and sit for my captain's ticket one day, imagine that?' Martin's eagerness brightened his eyes.

Kitty's heart lurched. Her anger deserted her as suddenly as it came; leaving her deflated and wrung out like a dishcloth. How proud would she be if he achieved that after what they had endured? Their parents would be so delighted one of their children had advanced themselves. She sighed. 'Well, it's your life, Martin. You must do as you see fit.'

'My trip is only to Hull this time. So, I'll be back in two days if everything goes according to plan. I'll come and see you then. I must be in London by the end of next week. Captain Peterson wants to meet with his crew a day or two before we sail.'

'Are you in an authoritative position then, son?' Max asked, absentmindedly stroking Rosie's hair.

'Yes, but there are a few men above me. I'm not sure as yet what position I'll have, but Captain Peterson told me he wants to train me. His other men are not as bright as he'd like. Oh, they know the sea like the back of their hands, but the Captain wants to train someone educated.' Martin grinned. 'Once we get to Australia, if the Captain's business goes well, there is a chance he will get another boat and that could be mine one day.'

Kitty arranged the cakes back on the plate. 'How did you meet this Captain?'

Martin lowered his gaze. 'I, er, met him in Hull about a month ago. The Captain helped me out of a…er, sticky situation with a…er…a female.' He twisted away to stare at the coals ablaze in the grate, his face flamed the same colour as the embers.

Max winked at Kitty and Clara giggled.

Martin left soon after, promising to be home again in two days, and Kitty sighed at the knowledge she had now lost two brothers. She just hoped she didn't lose Benjamin as well.

* * * *

Torrential rain bounced off the street as Kitty opened the tearooms for business the following morning. Grey autumn skies replaced summer blue and she sighed at the thought of facing another bleak winter. Alice suggested they should offer soup and hot pies as an alternative to sandwiches, now the weather grew cooler.

Kitty, Mary and Alice discussed this new idea when suddenly the back door was wrenched open and a very wet Mildred entered with Hetta close behind her.

'Ye Gods! That weather,' barked Hetta, shrugging off her coat. 'I'm soaked to the bone.'

'Soaked to the bone,' repeated Rosie from her chair at the table.

'I'll put the kettle on.' Mary chuckled. 'A nice hot cup of tea will fix you up in no time.'

'I hate the cold,' Hetta whined, tying on her apron. 'Me bones ache all the time an' then me chest. Oh, me chest hurts me so bad I have t'stay in bed. You wouldn't believe what I have t'go through.' Hetta kept on about her aches and pains, driving Kitty slightly mad with her moaning, but she knew deep down Hetta was a good woman with a big heart.

Urgent tapping upon the back door interrupted their talking. Mildred opened it and revealed a drenched, pimply youth.

'Miss McKenzie?' he wheezed, bending over to catch his breath.

Kitty frowned. 'Yes, I'm Miss McKenzie. Come in. Can I help you?'

'I was sent on before the others…to warn you.'

She closed her eyes. What had happened now?

'What you on about, lad?' Hetta placed her hands on her wide hips.

'Quiet, Hetta.' Kitty's heart turned over. She ushered the boy inside and closed the door. 'Tell me what has happened.'

'Mr Spencer has been 'urt at t'warehouse an' is bein' brought here. They're on their way now,' he said in a rush, his face red with the effort.

'Hurt? How bad? A scratch? A bump on the head?'

The boy lowered his lashes, not meeting her gaze. 'Real bad, Miss.' For a second no one moved, before the room erupted with chatter.

The women all stirred at once but went nowhere.

'Stop! Be quiet all of you. I cannot think.' Kitty turned to the boy again. 'Do you know where Dr Myers lives?'

''Tis all right, miss, the doctor's been sent for already.'

'Why was he not sent to hospital?'

'He asked to be tekken home. His last words before he passed out was he'd not die in a hospital.'

Kitty blinked and tried to organize her thoughts. She must prepare for the men bringing Max home,

AnneMarie Brear

but all she could think about was of him being hurt, and then Connie…

'I'll put water on to boil, miss,' Alice said, and added more coal to the range.

'Yes, good. Now Mary, go up and put an old blanket on top of Martin's bed. We will put Max in there for the doctor to attend to him. Then, tell Connie…that…that Max has met with a slight accident, but nothing too dreadful, just a few scratches and bruises. I don't want her worried.'

She looked at Mildred, who stood silent by the door leading into the tearoom. 'Mildred, you will have to see to the tearoom by yourself for a while. If it becomes too busy, which it might because of the rain, then call for Alice to assist you, and then you, Hetta,' here, Kitty twisted to the older woman, 'you will have to work the kitchen. Alice will show you what needs to be done, but you have been here long enough to manage, I'm sure?'

They all nodded.

A shout came from the courtyard.

Kitty opened the back door and rushed out into the teeming rain. A group of men held an old door between them bearing Max's large body covered by old, thin scraps of canvas. She didn't have time to look at him as the men puffed their way into the backroom. They paused for a moment to decide the best way to take Max upstairs, for there was no room to put him down in the busy backroom.

The staircase was too narrow to let the two men at the side go through, which left them standing in the hot kitchen. Their wet clothes steamed in the warmth. Alice thrust cups of hot sweet tea into their hands while Kitty followed the slow progress up the stairs.

Mary waited in the sitting room and showed the men where to take him. Obviously glad to be relieved of their burden, the men placed the stretcher on the floor beside Martin's bed and took the canvas off Max and then heaved the big man onto the bed.

Kitty rushed to Max's side. His low moans churned her stomach. Mary gasped at the mangled flesh and bloodied mess of Max's right leg. His misshapen right arm was clearly broken. Max's face, cut and scratched from his forehead down to his chin, also bore the brunt of the accident. His ripped shirt exposed deep cuts to his shoulder.

She glanced up at the workmen. 'How did this happen?'

The elder of the two men took his hat off and wiped his sodden forehead. 'The crane that carries goods from the boats t'warehouse broke an' it dropped its entire load. Max here pushed a young lad out of the way an' ended up coppin' most of it, yet he saved the lad from certain death.'

'Are you certain the doctor is on his way?'

'Aye.'

'I hope he arrives soon. Thank you for your help.' She nodded to the men and then looked at Mary. 'Take them down for some tea, and maybe find them a towel.' Kitty waited until they left the room before bending over Max's face and kissing his uninjured cheek. 'You'll be all right, Max dear, I promise.'

'Kitty. Kitty!' Connie's shouts startled Kitty and she dashed into her room.

'Where is he?' Connie struggled to get out of bed. 'Is he all right? Mary told me nowt.'

Kitty pushed her back against the pillows and straightened the blankets. 'There was an accident at the warehouse, but Max is fine. Some cargo landed on him. He has hurt his leg and scratched his face and shoulder.'

'I want ter see him.' Connie threw back the covers again.

'No, Connie. Stay in bed, please.'

'I want t'see for meself what he's like. You could be lying t'me,' puffed Connie, still trying to get out of bed even though her large stomach made it awkward.

'When have I ever lied to you? Now, stop it,' Kitty snapped. 'I cannot deal with the both of you.'

'Mrs Spencer, stop exhausting yourself and behave.' Doctor Myers stood in the doorway.

Kitty went to the doctor's side. 'Max is in the boys' room, Doctor.'

Mary brought up bowls of hot water and strips of cotton sheeting for bandages. The doctor, with Mary and Kitty's help, ministered to Max's injuries for over an hour before he was finally satisfied it was all they could do for the moment.

'He'll need to be watched constantly for the next few days.' The doctor frowned as he packed his bag. 'Someone will have to sit at night with him too. I'm fairly sure there are no internal injuries, but I cannot be completely positive. Bruising will come out once the swelling has gone down. I'll call back this evening.'

'You don't think he should be taken to the hospital?' Kitty asked. Her father once told her the poor feared hospitals as places of death, usually because by the time they waited to be ill enough to go to hospital, it was generally too late for the doctors to save them, but she felt Max needed to be there.

'Yes, he should really. But I'd rather not move him now. I believe we can manage him here well enough. I've no doubt we can give him constant attention, which is something he wouldn't always receive at the hospital. I shall review the situation in an hour or two. Now I must dash, I've two women in labour and have no idea which one to go to first.'

'Perhaps his leg needs an operation?' persisted Kitty, believing the doctor needed to pay more attention to this very important patient.

'No, it was a clean break like his arm. His leg looks terrible because of all the mangled flesh around the bone and the other cuts and tearing further up the thigh. It should heal properly in time now it's splinted. I'm more worried about either internal or head injuries. He may lapse into a coma. I shall consult with another doctor and be back as soon as I can. I'll ask for a report from the warehouse. I'm concerned about Mrs Spencer, Miss McKenzie. She is ready to have the baby at any moment and she needs to remain calm.'

'Very well.' Kitty sighed. 'Show Doctor Myers out please, Mary.'

Left alone, Kitty took a chair from the corner and brought it close to the bed.

'What a to-do,' lamented Hetta, carrying in a cup of tea for Kitty. 'Now, I don't want you ter worry a minute, Miss Kitty. I'll stay here tonight an' cook you all a meal an' see ter the bairns. You an' Mary will be far too busy tendin' ter Mr an' Mrs Spencer to worry about owt else.'

Kitty wanted to protest, as she didn't think she could put up with Hetta's chatter tonight. However, it would be easier to have someone attend to Rosie and keep Clara and Joe amused. 'Thank you, Hetta, I appreciate it.'

'Not a problem at all, Miss Kitty. I've got no one t'go home ter. So, I'll not be missed.'

Kitty stared at her and realized the poor woman was lonely. Hetta had no children and her husband and parents were long dead. The people under this roof were all she had for company. At fifty-eight years old, she was alone in a rented room in a tenement building. Compassion filled Kitty and she grasped the older woman's hand in acknowledgement before Hetta left the room.

Kitty rose and stepped to the window. The grey storm clouds still sent down their deluge. She shivered with cold. The room had no heating and she worried in case Max was cold too.

'How is he?' Connie appeared in the doorway, causing Kitty to nearly have a stroke.

Connie hobbled into the room and sat on the chair. 'Get back to bed,' Kitty whispered.

'Yes, I'll in a minute. I want t'see him first.'

'But Connie—'

''Tis all right, our lass. Me time is due now, so it won't matter if I start. But I had ter see Max. I'm beside meself with worry.' Connie took Max's right hand and kissed it. 'My, he's a mess.'

'The doctor said he'll mend in time.' She squeezed Connie's shoulder. 'Now go back to bed.'

'I nearly fell over the first time I put me feet on the floor. I thought I'd forgotten how to walk.' She shrugged, smiling through her tears. 'I just had ter see him, lass.'

'I know, dearest.' She planted a small kiss on top of Connie's head. 'Now, let us have you back in bed.' She helped Connie back into her bedroom.

'You'll come an' get me if he asks for me?'

'Of course, now rest.' Kitty smiled in reassurance and closed the door. She met Mary in the sitting room. 'Is everything all right downstairs?'

189

'Yes. Alice has Rosie occupied playing with scraps of pastry.'

'Good.'

Max's moans carried to them and they hurried into his room. His face had lost all colour and beads of sweat developed on his forehead. Kitty swiftly dampened a cloth and wiped them away. His breathing became laboured and she reached for the laudanum the doctor had left. She bit her lip as she measured out the right dosage and then tried to pour it into Max's mouth. Some of the mixture seeped past his lips and the rest dribbled down his chin. She hoped he swallowed enough to settle again. He groaned and coughed up blood. Her hands shook as she watched him. He looked ghastly.

'Poor Max.' Mary wiped away a tear.

'He is getting worse,' Kitty agonised. She felt his brow. 'He is hot one minute and then cold the next. He's sweating terribly and I think he's in pain, but he won't open his eyes.'

Max writhed and gasped for breath. His movement made blood ooze through the bandage on his shoulder.

Kitty groaned. 'He must stay still, or he'll tear his stitches.' She lifted off the blankets to check the bandages on his legs. She stilled.

Mary took a step closer. 'What's the matter?'

'Look,' Kitty whispered. She stared at Max's stomach and his exposed black hairy chest.

'At what…'

'Look under his hair, look through it. What do you see?' Mary peered at Max's chest and stomach. 'Bruises.'

'No, it is different, I have a feeling… Father used to take me sometimes to visit patients… I used to read his medical books, remember?' Her voice faltered. She twirled from the bed and dashed downstairs.

She didn't stop to grasp her hat or coat as she ran out of the back door and down the side path. Her hair came out of its confinement and whipped into her eyes.

She sprinted down the street, past people with open mouths as they realised who she was. She turned the corner and kept going. The cobblestones poked uncomfortably through her thin house slippers, but it didn't stop her. She kept running even when a stitch ached in her side. She lost her footing at times and stumbled but scrambled on.

The street the doctor lived on loomed before her. As she crossed the road, she was roughly grabbed by the arm and pulled back onto the walkway just as a carriage hurtled past. The cold wind from the passing carriage slapped her face.

'By God. What in hell's name were you trying to do, get yourself killed?' Doctor Myers ranted.

Kitty bent double, heaving. Only after she pulled her hair away from her face and he saw who he held in a vice grip did the doctor calm down.

'Miss McKenzie? What is it? The Spencers?'

'Max…' Kitty nodded, not able to speak. Her chest felt ready to burst as she dragged air into her lungs.

He took her by the arm and crossed the street to the hostelry on the corner. He told her to wait outside. After a few endless minutes, the doctor drove a horse and gig from around the back of the establishment. He reined in beside Kitty and she bundled into it without them speaking a word. Myers drove straight to the tearooms and Kitty mumbled for him not to wait for her but to go straight to Max. Instead, Dr

Myers hurried around to help her out. Together they rushed into the tearooms by the front entrance.

Dr Myers hustled her through to the back room. The silent weeping of Mildred and Hetta confronted them, halting them for a moment before they bounded upstairs.

Silence.

Kitty hesitated in the bedroom doorway as Dr Myers strode to Max. Alice sat on the chair, staring towards the bed. Beside the bed stood Mary, tears flowing unchecked down her cheeks. On the bed lay Connie, curled around Max as much as her huge stomach would allow.

Gently, Dr Myers examined Max where the blueness had seeped across his chest and stomach. Blood dribbled down his chin. 'Internal bleeding.' Myers bowed his head. 'I'm sorry.'

Kitty gasped and shoved her fist against her mouth to stop her groan. It was as though someone had punched her in the chest. She couldn't breathe. Some hideous weight pushed against her ribs. Max looked strangely content and her heart ached with acute pain.

Big beautiful Max, taken from them by a freak accident. Never again would they hear his loud booming voice, his laughter, his jokes or his stories. How many hours had he entertained the children in the cellar with his tales and games? But no more.

A sob caught in her throat. It was the only noise in the room. Connie lifted her head and gazed at her. The agony in her eyes made Kitty nearly double up in two. How will we all bear it?

* * * *

Kitty gazed around the tearoom at the people who stood or sat at tables sipping tea and eating sandwiches and cakes. It was a good turnout. They did Max proud. So many of his workmates and friends came to the graveside and most of them returned with the family for the wake. A good number of them had to stand in the backroom or in the courtyard due to the crowd. Poor Alice, Mildred and Hetta were run off their feet serving everyone; even Clara did her bit. Kitty gave her an encouraging smile as she passed by with a tray of sandwiches.

Kitty realized she hated the colour black. It dominated the room. Nearly everyone at the tearooms wore it. The girls had draped black material across the windows and tied black ribbons around each vase of flowers on every table. It seemed all colour had vanished. She wished to see something bright and gay and was thoroughly ashamed for thinking such thoughts on this terrible day.

Two days was all it had been. Two days. To Kitty it seemed like two years. Time had stood still since Max died, and she didn't know how they would move on without him. She gazed at Connie, sitting next to Dorothea and Mary. Despite her ordeal, she looked well, if very pale, as though she was enveloped in a peaceful aura.

Kitty trembled. Nothing more can happen to those I love, or I'll go raving mad.

'You all right?' Martin placed his hand on her shoulder.

She reached up and stroked his face. Today she would also lose her brother. A great sadness welled inside, threatening to choke her. She had to be brave.

'I'll be fine, dearest. What time does your train to London leave?'

'I'm not going.'

Kitty frowned. 'Not going?'

'No. I'll stay home. You'll need me now.'

Kitty straightened. 'Oh, no. No, Martin. You're leaving on that train today and sailing for a new life. One person in this family sacrificing their dreams is quite enough, I'll not let you do it too.'

'But without Max to help around the place and his wage, I thought—'

'No, Martin, no. You're going and I'll not argue about it.' She smiled to take the sting out of her words. 'I love you and I'll miss you, but I shan't let you stay here when so much out there waits for you. So, go. Pack your belongings and then come say goodbye to us all.' Kitty reached up and kissed his cheek. Oh, how I'll miss you.

Later that evening, Kitty and Connie sat on either side of the fire in the sitting room. With everyone in bed the hissing of the fire was the only sound.

Kitty gazed across the rim of her teacup at Connie and again received the impression Connie was at peace. Kitty wondered how she could be after losing Max. 'Are you very tired?'

Connie looked at her. 'No, lass.'

'Can I get you anything?'

'Nay, there's nowt you can get for me.'

Kitty hesitated. 'I think you have handled this nightmare extremely well, considering.' Her voice cracked with emotion. 'I admire you.'

Connie smiled. 'That's because I'm not frightened anymore.'

Puzzled, Kitty frowned. 'Frightened? Of what?'

194

'Of havin' this babby. You see, now Max is waitin' for us, I have no fear of dyin'.'

Appalled at this confession, Kitty stared. 'B-but you won't die, Connie, and neither will that baby.'

Connie turned back to stare at the fire. 'You can't guarantee it, our lass. Not that it matters, because Max'll tekk care of us. He had t'go first so he wouldn't be left behind.'

'I'll not listen to this kind of talk, Connie.' She took Connie's hand and squeezed it. 'Are you telling me you are willing yourself and that baby to die? Is that what you're telling me?'

Connie heaved herself up off the sofa and looked down at Kitty with a resolute expression. 'All I'm sayin' is, if either me or the babby die, then it'll be all right, because Max'll be there t'tekk care of us.'

'Well, it is not going to happen, and you have to believe that too.'

''Tis not up to either of us t'say what'll happen, only fate can decide.'

Connie leaned over and gave Kitty a peck on the cheek. 'Goodnight, lass.'

The night brought a cover of soft snow to the city of York. Winter was still a month away, but nature decided to bring an early warning to the townsfolk that the cold was here to stay for a long time. People rushed about a little bit quicker now, trying to complete their business so they could be indoors where it was warmer. The elderly complained of sore joints and achy bones at the thought of another long cold spell. While poor, harassed mothers wondered if they could manage to get another winter out of clothes already too short for their children and worn thin.

The first day of opening after Max's funeral proved busy. The cold weather gave people the excuse to call in for a cup of tea or bowl of tasty soup to warm them before they went on their way again. Alice made plenty of hot savoury pies and pasties, which proved just as popular as her cakes.

The back door opened as Hetta, with snowflakes casing her coat and hat, marched through carrying a wicker basket full of the family's freshly pressed clothes. 'It'll be a foot deep by nightfall, you mark my words!' She huffed, placing the basket on the floor and then removed her hat and coat. 'How are you all?' she greeted them. Not waiting for their reply, she went straight into a tale about one winter when it snowed for weeks on end trapping old people in their own homes.

'Stop your chatter, woman, and have some tea,' said Connie. Inching her way to the edge of her chair, she used the table as a support to help her stand.

'If you get any bigger, Mrs Spencer, you'll explode.' Hetta shook her head in disapproval.

'It ain't summat I've enjoyed.' Connie's eyes narrowed at the other woman. 'Do you think wearin' tents for clothes is fun?'

Kitty stepped between them and took Connie's arm. 'Are you going upstairs to rest? Dr Myers—'

'Is an idiot,' Connie scoffed. Unexpectedly, she groaned and lurched sideways.

'Connie!' Kitty eased her back onto the chair.

'Oh, lass.' Connie gazed down. A soaking stain spread through her skirts.

Everyone stared, mesmerized by the sight.

'I've been havin' an odd pain all night. Only, I thought it were just the babby lyin' funny.'

196

Mary came into the backroom with a customer order. 'What's happened?'

As though Mary's tone triggered something in their minds, they all moved at once in panic.

'Connie is having the baby.' Kitty wondered if her legs would hold her up, such was her anxiety. 'We must help her up to bed.'

Alice began filling up a large pot with water from the kettle. 'Hot water, we'll need hot water.'

Kitty, with Mary on the other side, helped Connie upstairs.

'We need the old towels to cover the sheets with, Mary,' Kitty instructed. She bit her bottom lip. For weeks she had been quietly organizing for this day and now that it had arrived, she was so nervous in case everything wouldn't go as smoothly as she planned. Connie's statement on the night of Max's funeral lingered on her mind.

Connie took hold of Kitty's hand. 'Listen. I want ter say this now in case I don't get the chance later.'

'No, Connie, please—'

'Listen ter me. No one knows the outcome, lass. So, I want you t'know that I love you. I love all of you, an' if I go ter be with Max an' the babby stays here, then will you tell it me an' its father loved it very much? Will you tell it that?' Her eyes begged Kitty.

Kitty nodded, her throat full. 'Come, let's get you comfortable. Then you can have a cup of tea. We've a long night ahead.'

Those words haunted Kitty as afternoon drew into evening and Connie only had the odd pain every hour or so.

By nearly eight o'clock, apart from constant backache, Connie suffered no more pains. Alice and her mother, Nora, the local midwife sat talking with Mary. Hetta, bless her kind soul, had taken Joe, Clara and Rosie home with her to save them from hearing Connie's moans.

'Well, Mrs Spencer.' Kitty grinned. 'How about a game of cards?'

'Aye, might as well, since nowt else…' Connie screwed up her face in pain.

Instantly, Kitty stroked her hand. 'Is it very bad?'

Connie's low groan caught the ears of the women in the sitting room. In seconds the bedroom was full. Nora went straight to Connie and rubbed her back as she arched upwards in pain.

'There now, lass, that's it, go with it. Well done,' Nora murmured.

The pain receded and Connie relaxed again. 'That was the worst one yet.'

'Obviously the little mite has decided to get a move on.' Nora nodded, smiling. 'I think you should try to sleep while you can.' She shooed everyone out again except Kitty, who sat back on the chair.

For the next three hours, Connie dozed between intense pains. The others sensed the labour was progressing and Alice, in her nervousness, had so much boiled water ready it made everyone laugh. Kitty asked Mary to sit with Connie while she went to wash and freshen herself.

In her bedroom, Kitty stood at the window and stared out along the street. New snow gave it a clean appearance. She knelt at the windowsill to pray to the unknown fates to spare Connie and her baby. 'God, I know I haven't been a dutiful believer, but I beg you to listen to me now. Let them live long and happy lives, please,' she whispered.

Opening her eyes, she rose with a feeling of calmness. As she washed her face and hands, her engagement ring glinted in the lamplight. Kitty kissed its emerald stone for luck and smiled. She missed Ben more this night than any other. She longed to see his smile and feel his arms around her, to hear his voice and see his eyes sparkle just for her. With a deep sigh, she straightened her shoulders and headed back to Connie and the fate awaiting them.

As the clock chimed one o'clock in the morning, Nora stood entrenched at the bottom of the bed. 'Right, now Mrs Spencer, do you feel like pushing at all?'

'Noooo!' Connie moaned through clenched teeth as a contraction peaked.

'That's fine. Just fine. You'll feel it when the time's right,' said Nora, watching the development between Connie's drawn-up legs.

Mary and Kitty, on either side of the bed, held Connie's hands and wiped her brow when needed.

'You're doing so well, dearest, so well.' Kitty encouraged her.

'I've had enough,' Connie puffed, her face wet with sweat.

'Soon it'll all be over, and your baby will be in your arms.' She helped Connie take a sip of water from a cup.

'No, no, it's tekkin' too long. It won't make it, I know.' Connie panicked as another pain seized her. She squeezed their hands until the blood stopped flowing, but Mary and Kitty ignored it as they helped her through the ordeal.

Over the rooftops the sky lightened in the distance, heralding a new dawn. Only, above the tearooms, Connie weakened. Half an hour earlier, Nora had sent

Alice for the doctor. Hours of constant contractions and pain had exhausted her.

Nora pulled Kitty to one side. 'I'm worried the baby is stuck or turned in the womb.'

'The doctor will know what to do, though?' Kitty whispered.

'Aye, but it's a tricky job. With the strength of her pains that babby should be out by now and it's just not happening.'

A groan from Connie, gripped by another contraction, interrupted them. This time there was a subtle change in her as nature took over. Connie grabbed her thighs and pushed. A guttural noise came from deep within her chest and she went red in the face from straining.

Beads of sweat broke out on Nora's forehead and her wispy grey hair stuck to it. She looked up from her position at the end of the bed. 'I can see the head, Mrs Spencer. That's good. Now, slow down, it's over for the minute, just take it easy.'

A bustle from the door announced Doctor Myers with Alice close behind him. He took in the situation then led Nora away a little so they could talk in private. Their attention was soon diverted back to Connie as she rose again to grip her legs and push. Doctor Myers talked her through it and praised her once it was over. He washed his hands and then felt her stomach. For some minutes he listened to and probed her extended mound.

'Twins, I think, Mrs Spencer,' he declared, before withdrawing to the end of the bed.

Connie, resting between pains, jerked at the doctor's words. 'Nay…'

'Twins,' Kitty and Mary spoke as one.

Connie stared at them in fear as another wave of pain descended on her.

'Right, Mrs Spencer, push hard now. We need to get these little ones out,' he said as the baby's head emerged. Quickly, he felt around its neck for the umbilical cord. At the next push, Dr. Meyers turned the shoulders and the baby slid onto the bed.

'It's a boy!' Kitty rushed up to kiss Connie's hot, red cheek.

'Is…he…alive?' croaked Connie.

As though sensing his mother's doubt, the tiny fellow roared out his fury at being unceremoniously wiped over with a warm cloth by Nora.

'Got a fine pair of lungs on him,' declared Nora, passing the scissors to the doctor for him to tie off and then cut the cord. Soon after, Nora picked the baby up and wrapped him in a soft woollen blanket. 'Come, Miss Mary. Hold this little one, for there is more work to be done.'

Tears formed in Mary's eyes as Nora gave her the baby. Slowly, she stepped to the bed and bent down to show Connie her first born, her son.

Connie raised her head to gaze in wonder at the tiny miracle. 'My son,' she whispered

'Oh, Connie, how beautiful is he?' Happiness and relief burst out of Kitty.

'He's as handsome as his dad.'

'I think you should get some rest before the next one makes its appearance, Mrs Spencer,' Dr. Myers murmured.

'I'll go make her a cup of tea,' Alice said rushing out.

Ten minutes later, Connie heaved and strained to push the next baby out. 'Wait, Mrs Spencer, wait,'

Myers instructed. 'The head is out but I must check for the cord.'

With the next contraction, Connie pushed.

'You have a daughter, Mrs Spencer. Congratulations.' Doctor Myers cleared the baby's airways of mucus.

'Is she all right?' Connie tried to sit up, anxious because the new baby hadn't cried.

Before the doctor could answer, the baby boy in Mary's arms cried and the tiny girl answered with her first wail.

Connie slumped back against the pillows and closed her eyes. ''Tis done, Max, I did it, me love.'

Only Kitty heard Connie's whisper. 'Connie!' Kitty, thinking she was slipping away from them, shook Connie's shoulders hard. Startled, Connie's eyes flew open. Kitty yelled into her face. 'Don't you dare leave me.'

'I'm tired, lass, so very tired,' mumbled Connie. 'What you yellin' for?'

Kitty bowed her head. Tears wavered on the edge of her lashes. 'I'm sorry. I thought…I…never mind.'

Doctor Myers peered over Connie's bent legs. 'Your job is not finished just yet, Mrs Spencer. There is the afterbirth. Then you can sleep the day away.' He smiled at her.

A short time later, Alice and Nora cleaned Connie and made the bed up with fresh sheets. Kitty sat with the baby girl in her arms beside Mary, who held the baby boy. They watched as Connie, dressed in a new nightgown, settled back against thick pillows and sipped a cup of tea.

'Two babies.' Kitty grinned at Connie. Her fear of losing Connie had receded now as good colour returned to her cheeks.

'What are they to be called then?' Nora asked, bundling the soiled sheets into a basket ready to take downstairs and boil.

'Charles an' Adelaide,' announced Connie. ''Tis a relief to finally say their names. I was plagued day an' night that this would end in nowt but disaster.'

Kitty gripped her hand. 'That is because you didn't listen to me.'

'My, they're fancy names and no mistake,' declared Nora. 'Right posh.'

Connie smiled. 'I had a lot of time t'look through Kitty's books while I was in bed for all those months. I was lookin' at one book about Australia, an' I noticed a town called Adelaide. I liked it an' so did Max.' Her bottom lip trembled.

'And Charles?' inquired Mary, holding the newly named Charles Spencer.

'Charles is Max's father's name. Max wanted it.' Connie dashed away her tears and sniffed.

'They are both fine names.' Kitty kissed Adelaide's soft downy head. 'I'm sure Max is smiling down, so proud of his babies.'

Chapter Fourteen

On New Year's Eve, just before midnight, Kitty sat holding Charles over her shoulder and rubbed his back. She often rose during the night to help Connie and found it strange how in the silence of night her thoughts grew depressing. As a fiancée in love with a good man she should be excited and blissful. Yet, her man was thousands of miles away, and his mother, the one woman whom in normal circumstances she should now regard as a second mother, disliked her. What a hopeless situation.

Kitty sighed and stared into the low twinkling fire. She ached to be held. Right now, she longed for her father's strong arms to hold her tight. She wished she could go to sleep listening to his stories of attending to the sick like she used to when her life was simple. But the men in her life had, one by one, left her—first her father, then Rory, Ben, Max and Martin. Each one was missed and left a burning hole in her heart.

The situation with Rory still saddened and angered her. No word from him in over a year hurt. Did he ever wonder about them? How could he behave in such a way? However, so much had happened without him that now she thought of him only in passing moments, as though he too had died like Max.

Charles snuffled into her neck and she hummed to him as Ben's smiling face came to mind. How could she miss him so much and still live? The constant ache she carried in her heart over him had strangely become a comfort.

Connie shifted Adelaide's weight as she nursed her. 'It's been a while since a letter arrived from Ben.'

'Yes, it has, over two months. It frightens me that his mother's venomous letters will work, and he'll think twice about me. I know I shouldn't doubt him, but sometimes I cannot help it. I also doubt myself and what we had.'

'Why?'

'I'm afraid of forgetting what he looks like. I fear he will forget me. He could easily fall for another, someone who is flesh and blood to him, whereas I'm merely a memory in a letter.'

'Nay, lass. He's true ter you. I know it.'

'I wish I had your confidence. I feel as though I've a weight on my shoulders that is pushing me down.'

Connie stroked Adelaide's small hand. 'What a funny old world we live in, lass.'

'Yes, it is.' Kitty nodded. 'Who would have thought the year would end as it has?'

'Mebbe there's a reason for it all?' Connie shrugged. 'Obviously it was meant t'be the way it was.'

'Well, we can only hope the New Year will be a great deal better.' She kissed Charles's cheek.

'It can be.'

'What do you mean?'

'Well, we can all go to Australia for a start, an' get you married ter that fellow of yours.'

Surprised, Kitty swivelled around to face Connie properly. 'Go...go to Australia?'

'Aye, why not? It's what you want, ain't it?'

'Well, yes. Yes, of course, but there are the others to consider and the shop and…'

Connie reached over and patted Kitty's hand. 'Listen, my lass, we've only one life t'live an' we never know when it's goin' to end. Haven't we learnt that recently? So, I say let's mekk the most of it.'

'I'll not go and leave you all here.' She shook her head, forestalling any argument.

Connie chuckled. 'No, our lass, you'll not be leaving any of us. We'll all go with you. The whole lot of us.'

Emotion caught at her throat. 'Do you mean it?'

'Aye, lass, 'tis time you were thought of first. Ben sounds so happy in his letters that it may be a while before he comes home. I think 'tis time you went to him instead.'

'But there is so much to consider.'

'As I see it, our lass, there's only one thing ter consider, an' that's startin' afresh. We've all had enough bad luck t'last us for a lifetime.'

'Oh, Connie.' Kitty let tears of joy and a little sadness fall freely.

They both grinned through their tears as the clock struck midnight and the twins burped in the New Year of eighteen hundred and sixty-six.

At breakfast, Kitty broke the news to her brother and sisters. Mary looked aghast, but Joe and Clara jumped up in excitement and Rosie clapped not knowing what was happening but glad to be included anyway.

'I can't believe you are doing this to us again,' stormed Mary, before rushing downstairs.

Connie raised her eyebrows. 'Stay strong.'

Kitty went downstairs to inform Alice. 'Alice, there is something I want to tell you.'

'Oh yes, Miss?' Alice smiled, glancing up from rolling out pastry. 'Mary ran out of here like a bullet from a gun—'

'Yes, but forget that for the moment. You see I have decided to sell the tearooms and emigrate to Australia to be with Benjamin and closer to Martin.' Kitty waited for her reaction.

Alice slowly straightened and with the back of a flour-covered hand she pushed away a blonde curl that had escaped her mop cap. 'Going to Australia?'

Kitty wrung her hands at the distress that flashed across the girl's face.

Alice nodded and plied her rolling pin without saying another word as the back door opened and Hetta and Mildred entered.

Seizing the moment before Hetta started her chatter, Kitty told them the same news.

Mildred's eyes widened in shock and she trembled a little. She excused herself to rush outside to the privy.

Hetta abruptly sat on a chair, threw her apron over her face and cried as though her heart would break.

The morning wore on, interspersed with bouts of Hetta breaking down in torrents of weeping and Alice making her endless cups of tea to soothe her. Kitty escaped upstairs at the earliest possibility to get away from the sombre atmosphere. No one talked much and even the trade wasn't as strong as usual. Mary returned home mid-afternoon cold and miserable. She went straight to her bedroom and shut the door.

Connie folded clean washing ready to iron. 'She'll come round sooner or later, lass.'

'I thought she would accept the news.' Kitty bit her bottom lip. 'I feel so guilty.'

'You can't keep living your life ter suit others.'

207

'But Ben may come home soon.'

'Aye, he could, an' then he could turn around six months later an' say he's goin' back. Which means we'd be going anyway. You've read his letters, lass. You know how happy he is. All he's missing is you.'

'Yes, I know you're right. Besides, Ben's home is Kingsley Manor. Eventually, we'll return to England.'

'Exactly, but for now, we've t'think of the future an' mebbe the future is a sunny new country where young 'uns can mekk a good life for themselves. I know that's what Max'd want for his babbies. That's why I suggested it. I have t'think what Max'd do, now t'twins are safely here. 'Tis me duty t'try an' give them the best I can.' Connie grinned a little self-consciously at her speech and Kitty smiled for the first time that day.

At supper, Kitty sat with the family to discuss the move.

'Why can't you go alone?' pleaded Mary. 'You can leave Connie, Alice and I to run the shop, it's not like we don't know how.'

'No, Mary. We all go together.' Connie crossed her arms. 'I think this family has been split up too much as it is.'

'But we are settled now. It's not like when we were in the cellar,' Mary continued to argue. She looked at Kitty. 'Why are you doing this to us again? You've gone back on your word.'

'Because what do we have here?' Kitty put her hands to her temples. 'What is left for us?'

Mary stood. 'You have the shop. Mr Kingsley will come back, and you will live in his manor.'

At the thought of living with Georgina, Kitty shuddered. 'In due course, yes, but for now I want to

208

be with him and experience another country. It will be good for all of us. Look at the trouble Joe got himself into. This can be a fresh start for us all. Why do you fight me, Mary?'

'I want to stay here. I'll run the shop myself.'

Kitty tutted. 'Don't talk silly. You're sixteen years old—'

'I'm old enough to know my mind!' Mary stormed into the bedroom and slammed the door.

Connie turned to Clara. 'Tekk Rosie and yourself off ter bed, me lass.' She looked at Joe. 'Night lad, I'll come tuck you in shortly.'

The three children kissed Kitty goodnight and she hugged them tightly. 'Sweet dreams.'

Once they had gone, Connie grasped Kitty's hand. 'What you thinkin' about?'

'I do not know if I'm doing the sensible thing.'

'What you mean?'

'I mean there is so much at stake. It all seems too exhausting to try and work out what is the correct thing to do at the moment. And lately, Rory has been popping up in my mind a great deal. Why, I do not know. He's been gone so long now. Nevertheless, I still think about him and wonder if he is all right, as much as it maddens me.'

'You shouldn't be wonderin' about him. He made his bed, lass.'

Kitty paced the floor. Her black skirts swished in the quietness of the room. 'I've not heard from Ben in over two months, not even a Christmas wish. I'm worried about selling the shop, packing everything and saying goodbye to people we know and care about. I could be making the biggest mistake of my life. It is going to be hard, Connie, really hard. I don't think I'm up to it.'

'You've made the decision now and it's the best one. I want you ter be happy, lass.' Connie reached over and extinguished the lamp's wick, plunging the corner of the room into darkness. 'You're tired, our lass, that's all. You've got ter stop gettin' up ter help me at night.'

Kitty placed the fireguard around the grate. 'No, Connie. I love being with the babies, it's the only time I have to spend time with them. Besides, you need help—'

'An' if I do, I'll wake Mary. You do enough durin' the day with the shop. I'll not argue with you,' Connie added, when Kitty was about to protest. 'Now get t'bed.'

'What am I to do about Mary?' 'Leave Mary to me.'

Connie rose before anyone else. The clock struck five as she dressed in her black crepe mourning dress and checked to make sure the babies slept soundly. After throwing her black shawl over her shoulders and slipping on her house shoes, she lit a candle and crept downstairs.

The back door opened just as Connie left the last step. Alice entered, shaking the snow off her hat and coat. 'Oh, Mrs Connie! You surprised me. Are the babies up?'

'No, lass, they're fast asleep. No, 'tis you I need t'see.'

'Me? Why?' Alice took off her coat and hat and removed her snow- encrusted boots to replace them with house slippers.

Connie opened the oven door and raked the embers with the poker before adding a few sticks of wood and some lumps of coal. 'I want ter talk ter you

AnneMarie Brear

about Kitty. She's under too much pressure an' worries about everyone an' everything. She's goin' ter mekk herself ill.'

Alice put on her apron and then lit a few more lamps positioned around the room, giving the backroom extra light for her to cook by until the sun came up. 'What did you have in mind?'

Connie lifted the large black kettle full of water onto the stove plate. 'Will you write a letter for me ter Mrs Cannon? Me writin' is like hen scratchings.'

'Aye, but why? What can Mrs Cannon do?'

'I'm not sure until I can have a word with her, but more than likely she'll have an answer. Her bein' a smart woman.'

Quickly, they composed a letter before Kitty rose. Then, Alice changed back into her outdoor clothes and ran down the street to look for a cab to deliver the message to Dorothea.

'How are you going to talk to Mrs Cannon in private without Kitty knowing?' Alice asked on returning.

'Kitty goes t'bank today. I'll get her ter do some shoppin' for me as well an' that'll keep her out longer.'

At eleven o'clock, Kitty left the tearooms and Connie sighed with relief when no more than two minutes afterwards Dorothea Cannon's carriage swayed to a halt in front of the tearooms. Mildred opened the door for her, and, with a smile, Dorothea sailed through into the backroom.

'Morning, Mrs Cannon,' said Alice, bringing from the oven a tray of hot mince pies.

'Good morning, Alice. My, they smell delicious! I'll buy some to take home with me, if I may?'

211

Dorothea pulled off her gloves. She unhooked her sable-lined cloak and gave it to Mildred. 'How are you, Connie?'

'Well enough, thanks, Mrs Cannon.' Connie smiled. 'Shall we go upstairs?'

'Of course.' Dorothea followed her to the rooms above and sat on the sofa in front of the blazing fire.

Connie sniffed. Nerves threatened to unsettle the good breakfast she had eaten hours before. 'Thank you, Mrs Cannon, for answerin' me message.'

'As if I wouldn't,' admonished Dorothea. 'So, you are worried about Kitty? Is she doing too much?' Dorothea's intelligent blue eyes were full of concern.

'It's not her physical health I'm worried about, though she's as thin as a rake. No, it's more like her mind.' Connie stabbed at the fire with the iron poker. 'So much has happened ter her in such a short time. She has everythin' on her shoulders an' she doesn't like t'share the load.'

'I agree. However, Kitty is of strong spirit.'

'Aye, she is, but she's not happy an' she deserves ter be.' Connie swallowed, gathering her courage. Never had she asked for a favour before. 'Kitty needs ter go ter Mr Kingsley, but Mary is mekkin' her feel guilty for goin' back on her word.'

'Mary has to be shown that not everything is black and white.'

'Aye. I'm doin' me best ter talk her 'round.' Connie sighed deeply. ''As Kitty sent you a note about us leavin'?'

'Yes. It arrived yesterday. I wasn't surprised. She cannot wait forever for Benjamin to come home. He is enjoying Australia and is not likely to return soon. Of course, I'm sure he misses Kitty sorely, but he is a young man on adventure. My son-in-law, John, told me only two days ago that Benjamin has accomplished everything he needed to concerning the business and now he is pleasing himself by joining exploration expeditions in the desert. John is worried because Benjamin shows no signs of returning soon. I think if John's health was better, he would travel there himself to keep an eye on him. We cannot afford to lose the only Kingsley heir.' Dorothea paused as Mildred entered carrying a tea tray and Connie stood to serve.

After Mildred left and the tea was handed out, Connie sat back down and sighed. 'Max didn't want ter go ter Australia when Kitty first mentioned it. He was afraid he'd be too old ter get work, but now I know he'd want me ter tekk the twins an' start a new life an' give them the chance of betterin' themselves. They'll not get that here. I don't want Charles ter work down a pit or in a warehouse, or Adelaide marryin' someone who drinks his wages away an' gives her a black eye each Friday night an' a babby every year.' Connie blushed, realising her conversation was too direct for someone of Dorothea's standing.

Dorothea leaned over and patted her hand. 'I want Kitty to go and marry my grandson. I want it very much and so I'll do all in my power to make it possible. I know it's been hard for her. First, her parents' deaths and finding out she must support her brothers and sisters with no income, then her oldest brother leaving her to cope alone. Kitty has told me many times that without your and your late husband's help they wouldn't be here now.'

Connie sniffed again. ''Tis nowt we've done, she done it on her own. Besides, she's family now.'

213

Dorothea sipped her tea and then replaced her cup back on its saucer. 'My daughter, Georgina, will not be pleased at this news of Kitty joining Benjamin. I have to be careful in how this business is transacted.'

Connie blinked. 'Pardon?'

'Georgina must not hear of Kitty's plans. I shall confer with John.' Dorothea gave a final pat to Connie's hand. 'Leave it all too me. All will be well, and I know John will help too. So, don't worry anymore about it. I'll start organising this trip first thing in the morning.'

* * * *

During the following week nothing was said about moving or even starting to put the process in motion.

Kitty went about her daily tasks of running the tearooms and seeing to the needs of her family. She'd tried to talk to Mary but received the cold shoulder every time. This coolness made Kitty hesitate to put a 'For Sale' advertisement in the paper.

In the middle of January, a parcel arrived from Ben. Elation sang in Kitty's veins as she opened it and read the letter. The parcel also contained an etching of Sydney harbour and after admiring it, she passed it around the family, who gathered close. She then pulled out a likeness of Ben done in oils. Unprepared for such a surprise, she gasped at his beautiful face. His cornflower eyes smiled just for her and she staggered under the enormity of sensation that swamped her. A sob broke through the restriction in her throat. Hugging the portrait to her chest, she rocked back and forth before gazing down on the painting again.

'Oh, Ben, my darling Ben.' Her tears splashed his face and she hurriedly dabbed them off.

'Come, lass,' Connie soothed. 'Come sit down.'

Kitty spun in her arms, her face awash. 'I miss him, Connie. I miss him.'

'I know, lass, an' that's why we're leavin' here so you can be with him.'

'I promised Mary we would stay.' She stumbled to a chair and sat, still clutching Ben's likeness.

'So much has happened since then.' Connie scowled at Mary, who stood behind Kitty.

Mary wiped away a tear. 'I'm sorry, Kitty. I should not have made you choose.' Kneeling before her, Mary took both of her hands in her own. 'Kitty?'

Kitty gazed down into Mary's eyes. Tears blurred her vision. 'Yes, pet?'

'Let us start packing in the morning. I long to see all those beautiful birds Ben writes so much about, don't you?' Mary smiled.

'Aye, 'tis time for a change,' Connie answered for them all. ''Tis time we all claimed a bit of happiness. I think Max would agree too.' She wiped a solitary tear from her cheek. 'I know I need a change of scenery.'

Mary fished a handkerchief from her pocket and mopped Kitty's face. 'I'm sorry.'

Kitty clasped her hand. 'I'll make sure we're happy. Every day, I'll strive to make it happen.'

Mary stood and kissed her. 'I know you will.'

'Right then.' Connie put her hands on her hips. 'We best mekk a start about leaving. Go wash your face and do your hair, lass. You've got ter make a trip ter Mrs Cannon's place, for she's already got a buyer for the tearooms.'

Kitty reared back. 'A buyer? Already?'

'Aye, a few days ago. Nowt were said because of how you were feelin'. An' Mr Kingsley has some papers for you t'look over. So, you've a journey ter his place an' all.'

'Oh, no, Connie. I won't go near Georgina Kingsley.' The thought of facing that woman again made her skin crawl.

''Tis fine, lass, she's in London for the month. Mrs Cannon told me last week. Mr Kingsley has been wantin' to see you for a while, but he's been poorly.'

'You know a great deal.' Kitty blinked rapidly to clear her head. 'You must have very been busy behind my back, Mrs Spencer.'

'Aye, we have, our lass, but it's always been for your benefit.' Connie chuckled, giving Kitty's shoulder a squeeze. She winked and went to see to her babies.

Clattering up Kingsley Manor's drive, Kitty was transported back to the sunny day last spring when Ben took her to meet his parents. Shuddering in her thick black woollen coat, not from cold, but at the memory of that first frosty meeting with Georgina, Kitty was glad today she wouldn't have to face her.

She gazed out the cab's window at the passing snow-covered garden beds and thought of the last few hours she had spent with Dorothea at Cannonvale Park, on the outskirts of York. The speed at which plans were being made shocked her. Dorothea told her of the buyer for the tearooms, a friend of a friend, and about the generous amount he offered for the business and living quarters above.

Kitty twitched the reticule on her lap. It bore a list of things needing to be done in the coming weeks, plus the booking information Dorothea gave her of a well-respected ship and its captain. All was in hand and she allowed a tiny spark of happiness to glow in her heart. Her new life would soon begin.

Alighting at the door, she smiled at the butler who guided her into the drawing room. While he went to inform Mr Kingsley, she gazed around the large, beautifully ornate room. She strolled over to study a painting of a cavalier high up on the wall, taking her gloves off as she did so. Abruptly, she heard Georgina's voice echo in the hall and cringed.

'Was that a carriage at the door, Ticklewaite?'

'Er, a cab, Madam. Miss McKenzie is here to see the master.'

'My husband is busy, Ticklewaite. I shall speak to Miss McKenzie, continue with your duties.'

Kitty groaned and turned for the door. She had no wish to greet Ben's mother.

'Well, this is a surprise, I must say.' Georgina Kingsley's voice trilled around the drawing room. Her alabaster face was a stark match for her deep ruby dress. She looked drained of all blood.

Kitty straightened her shoulders ready for her attack. 'Mrs Kingsley.' She inclined her head in acknowledgement. 'I did not expect to see you.'

'So, you thought you would sneak into my house and visit my husband, did you?' Her eyes narrowed. 'Have you set your designs on him now, is that it? Isn't my son good enough for you? Do you prefer to corrupt the one who holds the money instead of waiting for him to die and for Benjamin to inherit?'

'Your vile accusations are beneath comment. I'm simply here to speak with your husband on issues that do not concern you.'

'I'm afraid he is too busy to see you at present.' Georgina sauntered further into the room and sat on the edge of a chair upholstered in gold chintz. Her whole demeanour showed condemnation. Her lips had thinned into a tight line. 'You should have sent word of your intentions, but perhaps I can help you?'

'No, I do not think so, but I thank you for your offer.' Kitty pulled on her gloves and walked towards the door. She had to leave this house and that woman's presence before she lost her temper altogether.

'Would you care for some tea, Miss McKenzie? I'm sure we can find something to talk about,' Georgina said with false sweetness.

Kitty stared at her, amazed at the woman's easy transformation. What a fine actor she was. Suddenly, Kitty smiled. No longer did Georgina cast a shadow over her and Benjamin's happiness. Soon, they would be together, married and away from her influence. The freedom of this newfound confidence invigorated her. 'I'm certain we both have more interesting things to attend to.'

'Do you still receive letters from my son?' The words were ground out.

Kitty's smile widened. 'Indeed, yes. Beautiful letters.'

'There are most probably a dozen or so women who receive such letters from my son.' Georgina's hands clenched. 'He has a way with women. They simply swoon at his feet. He has admirers all over the country.'

'But only one wears his grandmother's ring.'

218

Georgina sprang to her feet. 'And do you believe that is all you need to secure my son?'

'His love is enough for me.'

'You are deluded. I'll never allow your filthy family to join mine.'

'How dare you. You consider yourself so superior—'

'I'm superior! Your mother whored herself to pay for her debts because your father chose to attend to the poor instead of his own class.'

A red mist of anger clouded Kitty's senses. 'Lair. What do you know of my parents? You never knew them.'

'Yes, I did. I graced a few of the same social gatherings that your parents wormed their way into. Everyone knew they were beneath us.' Georgina straightened and raised her chin to sneer. 'Your parents had a name, did you know that?'

Kitty shook her head. 'I'll not listen to your evilness.'

'The Pretenders, that was their name.' Georgina's gaze raked over Kitty, making her feel like something repulsive. 'They pretended to be of a class they weren't, and it seems you are continuing the trade by whoring yourself to my son for his wealth.'

Kitty stepped closer to the dragon of a woman but resisted the urge to scratch her eyes out. Instead, she slowly smiled and lifted her chin. 'Like it or not, your son loves me. It is I who will bear the next generation and heirs for Kingsley Manor. You should think twice before making an enemy of me.'

Georgina's eyelid twitched. 'I'd rather him dead than be with you.'

'Kitty!' John Kingsley strode into the room. 'Why, my dear, it is marvellous to see you. We do not see you enough. Do we, Georgina?'

John's appearance alarmed Kitty. He was thin and pale, more so since she saw him last. Going to him, she took his hands and kissed each of his cheeks. 'How are you, Mr Kingsley?'

'I'll be much better when you call me Father,' he joked. John gently pulled her to his side and turned to his wife. 'Excuse us, my dear. I have some business to discuss with Kitty. We shan't be long.'

They left the open-mouthed Georgina and went down the hall to John's study where he showed Kitty to a large, dark brown leather chair near his desk before he sat on the other side. 'I'm glad you came. I was ready to send you a note.'

'Has something happened?' Kitty panicked. 'Do you know something about Ben that I don't?'

'No, no, dear. Benjamin was fine the last I heard,' John assured her. 'Dorothea has been my informant concerning you, since my business interests keep me too busy to see you regularly myself and, of course, my health is a weary burden also. I hope you don't mind that we have discussed you at times?'

'No, not at all. I'm glad you think so well of me.' Her cheeks grew hot. John leaned back in his chair, smiling at her. 'You are soon to be my daughter-in-law. I know Benjamin has made the correct choice and so I care for you already.'

'Thank you,' Kitty said, overcome with emotion. How could a woman such as Georgina have a wonderful husband like John?

'Now, down to business.' From a drawer, he pulled out sheets of parchment paper and rolls of documents and sorted through them. While he did this, Kitty looked around the room. Dark mahogany furniture and walls covered in rich, red silk wallpaper made the room masculine. Oil paintings of country and hunting scenes hung at intervals between tall bookcases. A small fire glowed in the grate and she realized this room was special to John.

'I would like to ask a favour of you, my dear.'

She nodded. 'Yes, certainly.'

'These documents are different business concerns, but this larger one is very important as it's my last will and testament. They are copies of the originals kept by my solicitor. Please would you take them and give them to Benjamin. He needs to know what I have arranged for his inheritance.'

'But, Mr Kingsley, you can hand these to Ben. He would...' Kitty's voice faded as John held up his hand to silence her.

'My dear, if I could I'd be on the next ship to Australia to be with my son and witness your marriage, but alas, my health is such that I'm lucky to still be alive today.'

'Mr Kingsley, you do look a little wan and thinner, but not at death's door surely?'

John stepped round the desk to pick up one of her hands. 'I've had two major heart seizures and a lot of little ones in between. The doctors tells me that my next one will be the end. So, I have to arrange my affairs bearing that eventuality in mind.'

She tried to hide her despair. 'But it may not happen for some time.'

'I'm in constant pain. I have accepted it.' He left her to sit behind his desk. 'You see this?' John tugged a small steel chest across the desk. It was ordinarily plain, measuring one foot by two foot. He extracted a small set of keys from his waistcoat pocket. Selecting one of the keys, he opened the chest's lock and lifted the lid back.

Her eyes widened at numerous small velvet bags inside. Each dark blue velvet bag was tied with gold cord. On the side of every bag were the initials B.K. stitched in gold thread. Kitty gazed up at John. The whole performance reminded her of the money she and Connie found in Martha's sofa. Her skin rose with goose bumps.

'There are twenty bags in this chest. Each bag holds ten gold sovereigns. They have been collected for Benjamin's wedding day since the day he was born, thirty years ago. It is a tradition in my family as far back as ancient times, apparently. My father continued it when I was born and on my wedding day, he gave me this very same chest full of bags of money. Sovereigns are added on special days, like birthdays, or a first tooth, first day in long pants, first time one writes one's name and so on.' John paused and wiped the moisture from his eyes with a linen handkerchief. 'I shall not be able to give this chest to Benjamin in person. I ask you to take this chest and give it to my son and tell him I love him and am so proud of him.' John's voice trembled with emotion. Kitty left her chair and went to him. Hugging each other tightly, Kitty whispered her promise to him.

* * * *

Nine days later, Kitty and the family were in the middle of packing. She had sold off what furniture she didn't want to take or that the new owner didn't want to have.

In her bedroom, Kitty folded clothes into a trunk. As she sorted and packed her eyes strayed to the newspaper lying on her bed. For the last two weeks she'd placed advertisements in the paper for Rory to get in contact with her. Depressingly, she'd received no answer.

She glanced up as Mary entered carrying a folded piece of paper. 'This just arrived for you from Mrs Cannon's driver.' Mary gave her the sheet.

'Oh, and Alice wishes to speak to you when you are finished here.' She hopped from one foot to another, excited. 'I think she wants to come to Australia with us.'

'Really?'

Mary grasped Kitty's wrists. 'I think both she and Hetta wish to join us. May they?'

Surprised, Kitty grinned and shrugged. 'If they really wish to then yes, of course.'

Mary squealed and ran from the room. Smiling, Kitty opened the note.

Dearest Kitty,

I shall be brief for time is against me as I'm needed at every turn.

John died last night. His heart gave out during an argument with Georgina as I understand it.

I'm at Kingsley Manor for the foreseeable future. You must not visit me here as I feel the consequences would be dire for yourself and Georgina.

The doctor fears for her sanity.

I'll write again soon with regards to our plans.

D.

Kitty bit her lip. Poor Mr Kingsley. She gazed at her engagement ring and thought of Ben. It would be months before he knew his father had died. She read the note again and shivered in response to Dorothea's warning. Don't worry, Dorothea, I have no wish to see Georgina ever again.

On the first Saturday in March, coral streaks brightened the sky over York as Kitty roused the family awake. Their cold breakfast was a hurried affair and the washing up even quicker. They wrapped the last of the tableware in sheets and blankets off the beds and packed them tightly into the last trunk to be locked. The packed tea chests had already been sent ahead to the ship at Liverpool. All the other luggage was piled in the backroom.

Joe, Clara and Rosie, beside themselves with excitement, were shooed downstairs to watch for Dorothea's carriages.

By eight o'clock, the babies were fed, washed and changed into clean clothes to keep them settled for the beginning of the train journey to Liverpool. Hetta arrived carrying a large carpetbag and a neighbour's young lad carried a small trunk that he deposited on the walkway in front of the tearooms.

With Hetta and Mary's help, Kitty packed away every last item. The books she'd read about emigrating said they would need plenty of home comforts and even food to supplement the ship's fare, even though they travelled first-class and not second-class or steerage, thanks to Dorothea's financial aid. Nevertheless, she didn't want to take any chances and would rather have too much, than not enough.

Dorothea's carriages rolled to a halt at the front of the tearooms a short time later. 'Good morning,

everyone!' she cried on descending the carriage step.
'We are right on time.' Turning to the three carriage
drivers, she asked them to begin loading the luggage.
'Is this not exciting?' She patted Clara's cheek.

'I wish you could come on the ship with us, Mrs
Cannon,' Clara said.

'Well, I'm going with you as far as the dock, that
is something for a woman of my age, do you not
agree?' Dorothea grinned.

Joe hopped about, unable to stand still. 'Will our
ship be the biggest there do you think, Mrs Cannon?'

'Oh, no doubt about it, my sweet.' Dorothea
laughed at him. 'Now we must hurry, for we have a
train to catch.'

Once the carriages were loaded and the children
aboard, Kitty closed the front door of the tearooms
and slid the lock into place for the final time. She
swallowed her tears. 'Well, there is an end to it.'

'Just on a year, lass.' Connie squeezed Kitty's
hand. 'That's all we've been here for, but it feels
much longer.'

'Well, at least we didn't go under. And there were
times when I thought we would.'

'You did yourself proud, my dear.' Dorothea
smiled. 'You made something out of nothing and not
everyone can do that. You all did extremely well.'

'It couldn't have happened without you, Dorothea.
Your friendship and patronage were invaluable to all
of us, and it'll never be forgotten.' Kitty kissed the
old woman's cheek.

She turned to Alice who came in from the
backroom. 'Good morning, Alice. How was it saying
goodbye to your family?' Alice's red eyes from
weeping told the story and Kitty gave her a quick
hug.

'Isn't any of your family coming to the station, dear?' asked Dorothea.

Alice's bottom lip trembled. 'God, no, madam. I couldn't go through all that again.'

After ushering everyone out the back door, Kitty lingered in the tearooms. She was leaving all this for an unknown future on the other side of the world. For a moment terror filled her. Yet, beneath the terror lay a bud of excitement and hope. 'Goodbye, dear rooms. You served us well.'

She walked into the backroom, a room usually warm from the ovens and noisy from the hustle and bustle of the women who worked in it. Now it was dim, cold and bare of all comfort. Smiling through her tears, she glanced around for the last time before she closed and locked the door.

She walked across the courtyard, through the side gate and up the lane to the street. The horses tossed their heads as they waited. In the crisp morning air, their nostrils blew out shots of steam. Her large family peeped out the carriage windows grinning at her. She smiled and went to the first carriage, which she shared with Dorothea, Mary and Rosie. The driver waited to hand her in, but she held back for a moment.

Kitty looked up at the front of the tearooms and stored the image in her memory. Suddenly, she craned her neck to stare down the length of the street. For some reason she needed to make sure Rory wasn't standing there. Something inside told her to check he wasn't calling for her to wait for him. She imagined she heard his footsteps on the dark cobbles. For a moment she wavered. How could she possibly leave York without getting word to him?

'Kitty, dear, it is time,' Dorothea said. 'Are you all right?'

'Yes. Yes, I'm fine. It was ghosts, that is all.' Kitty sat beside her and smiled at Mary and Rosie opposite.

'You know that with my contacts I tried to find Rory for you?' Dorothea whispered.

Kitty nodded, leaning back against the upholstery of the carriage seat as it rolled slowly away from the tearooms. 'I know. It's just…I never stop missing him.'

Dorothea patted her hand. 'He made his choice, my dear. You cannot live his life for him, remember that.'

Kitty turned her head to stare out the window. To each street they travelled along she bade a silent farewell. Who knew what the future held for her and her family? It was a sobering thought as they passed the cemetery where Max, her parents and sister lay. They didn't stop the carriages to say a last goodbye, having paid a visit earlier in the week. Besides, enough tears had been shed. It was time to look forward. Time to grab the future and take a strong hold.

Farewell, York, city of our births, and goodbye.

Chapter Fifteen

Kitty leaned over the wharf's iron rails and sniffed the salt air. Below, the murky water of the Mersey slapped against the quay's wood and stone support structures. She spun around and leaned back against the railing to scan the busiest port throughout the world, Liverpool. Anticipation gripped her. She feasted on the scene. People came here from all over Europe, only to leave again on ships from this very port and start anew in other countries. A walk along the quays highlighted the different nationalities, as folk huddled together waiting for their turn to board the vessels taking them even further away from their homelands.

Strolling along the dock, Kitty listened to the foreign languages and admired the national dress of countries she dreamed about. Groups of each nationality merged together with their meagre belongings and spoke in hushed tones of their own language. Fear tinged the atmosphere. Their trepidation of the unknown could be clearly expressed without a word of English being uttered. No loving family members came to say farewell to these pitiful groups, for their relatives were already thousands of miles away.

Kitty meandered until she came to the bustle surrounding the iron-built ship, the Ira Jayne, a vessel containing both steam engine and sails. It would be

228

taking her and her extended family from the shores of England across the great oceans of the world to the land of their new beginning.

The captain, Mr Bartholomew Curtin, was a friend of a friend of Dorothea's. Therefore, as a matter of priority, Dorothea secured first- class cabins for Kitty's party. Their luggage had already been installed in the hold a week before. Tomorrow morning they'd be piloted down the River Mersey and out into the Irish Sea to steam or sail away as the wind allowed.

But, for the moment, she had the opportunity to stretch her legs one more time before being cooped up on the ship for months. The docks spectacularly assaulted every one of her senses. Her gaze swivelled to take everything in, her ears buzzed with sound. Seamen worked in the ship's rigging at dizzying heights, while others loaded crates and chests tied on to swinging pulleys and then heaved onto the ship. Shouts and commands pierced the air. To her untrained eye it seemed to be chaos, an organized chaos, but chaos all the same.

A great commotion and noise occupied the wharf as the steerage passengers trudged aboard. Fathers, with furrowed brows, hustled their wives and children. Clutching what little luggage they owned, they followed the seamen trustingly. The English families cried, broken-hearted, waving handkerchiefs to loved ones they would never see again.

Kitty's throat constricted with emotion. Her thoughts flew to Rory. Will I ever see him again? He didn't even know they were leaving the country. Had she failed her parents? Was the promise she made at their graveside false? Despite all her best efforts, the family was divided, split asunder, but it wasn't floundering, not really. Yes, Rory had absconded, breaking her heart, but it'd been his choice. Just like it'd been his choice to stay away.

Shrugging, she sighed back her disappointment and concentrated on the future. She was still responsible for so many lives, for their happiness and security. Yet, she would have help. She wasn't alone. Besides Connie, she had Ben, the man who loved her.

At the foot of the gangplank leading up to the deck, she paused. Once she walked onto the ship, she'd be leaving English soil for an uncertain length of time, perhaps forever. Everyone was aboard waiting for her to finish taking this last stroll, but still she hesitated.

She looked back over her shoulder at the skyline of Liverpool and, somewhere in the east, York lay. She was saying goodbye to her old home, her country, her brother and heading on an adventure that would test her spirit and courage.

She heard her name being called and looked up at the ship to see Joe waving to her, beside him stood Dorothea, waiting to say goodbye to them all.

Taking a deep breath, she slowly walked up to the deck into Dorothea's waiting arms.

'I shall miss you more than I thought possible, my dear,' Dorothea told her.

They stood on the lower deck of the ship staring back at the crowded dock. The family, restless and eager, paraded around the poop deck above.

'What would I have done without you?' murmured Kitty. 'We wouldn't be where we are today if not for your influence.'

'Nonsense! You are made of stern stuff, my dear. You'd have survived with or without me.'

'No, Dorothea, no I wouldn't. Without you, the shop would've gone under, Joe would still be in gaol and Georgina would have found a way to drive Ben and me apart.'

Dorothea patted Kitty's hand and dabbed her eyes with her handkerchief.

'I love you very much.' Kitty smiled through her tears, hugging the old woman to her.

'I feel the same about you, my dear. Before I met you, I lived a very dull life.'

'I find that hard to believe.' Kitty chuckled, wiping her eyes. 'Will you think about coming over to see us some time?'

'Maybe, but I'm old, dear. Nonetheless, I may make the trip with Georgina, after she has recovered from her loss. No doubt, she will wish to see Benjamin soon. I would also like to see him again.'

'Benjamin would be so thrilled if you did. You mean so much to him.' She refrained from mentioning Georgina. The woman had no warmth in her heart.

Dorothea held Kitty by the shoulders. 'Soon there will be other things for my grandson to treasure, such as a wife and children. That is all a man needs. A happy and loving home life far outweighs anything else. Remember that, my dear, and you will both be very happy. And promise me to bring him home again soon, will you?'

'Yes, I promise.'

A whistle blew and a command ordered all visitors to leave the ship before the Captain boarded. Kitty and Dorothea joined the others and the farewells began. After a last hug to Kitty, Dorothea allowed a seaman to aid her down the gangway. From her carriage step, she waved and then drove away.

On the drifting evening breeze, with the sun descending into the orange-streaked horizon, the officers lined up to welcome the captain on board.

Kitty waited on deck with the others as the ropes were cast off. The sun was descending, casting an orange glow across the water.

It took a long time for the ship to slowly head down the river Mersey. Kitty returned the waves of the few strangers left on the docks and her heart thumped against her ribs as the dark buildings inched further and further away. All the passengers stood side by side on the decks, their tears and farewells mixed with the thrill of witnessing something different.

It took some time to reach the mouth of the Mersey, though none of the English passengers minded as it was their last view of English townships and countryside, even if all they saw were twinkling lights and dark outlines. Nevertheless, saying goodbye to their homeland, maybe for the last time, was not to be missed. It didn't matter if they weren't from Liverpool. It was English soil.

Finally, the pilot handed the control of the ship to the captain and was ferried away in a small boat. The dying wind kept the sails furled and so under steam they entered the Irish Sea and headed along the coast of Wales.

Weary and aching with cold, Connie ushered the exhausted family to their beds to sleep their first night on the water, leaving Kitty to stand alone by the rail.

Darkness had claimed both land and sea. A full moon shone on the inky black waters. The cool breeze made little bumps rise on her skin, but it also brought her the drifting sounds, the flapping of the sails, ropes squeaking in the wind, of a haunting melody sung by a lone seaman and the deck boards creaking as the ship swayed with the swell. She shivered and pulled the shawl around her tighter as she rested against the rail.

She stared up at the black expanse of the sky, bejewelled with the glittering stars. How many nights would she gaze at the stars before she was in Ben's arms?

Now the ship had set its course, the sailor's activity had lessened. One seaman walked by carrying rope over his shoulder and inclined his head in her direction.

'Evening, Miss.'

'Good evening.' She smiled.

His kind, weather-beaten face creased in concern. 'It's getting cold, you might want to go down below.'

'Yes, I will.'

'Soon though we'll be in the tropics and the heat will cook us,' he joked.

'Have you been to Australia before?'

'Oh yes, many times, Miss.' He scratched his head under his cap. 'Grand place if you want to start again and get ahead. There's lots of opportunities for folk there, I've heard.'

She nodded, her heart lifting. 'I heard the same.'

'Well, miss, if you've the courage to take chances, you'll do well out there.'

'I've become used to taking chances.' Kitty grinned and turned to grip the rail, fired up with enthusiasm. With Ben by her side there'd be nothing they couldn't achieve.

'Soon, Ben,' she whispered into the breeze. 'I'll be with you soon.'

Kitty McKenzie's saga continues in the sequel - *Kitty McKenzie's Land.*
Kitty McKenzie's path has taken her from the slums of York to the inhospitable bush of colonial Australia. Yet, when she believes her dreams will never be attained, she is shown that sometimes life can be even better than what you wish for.
The sequel is available in Kindle & paperback, large print and audio.
http://myBook.to/KittyMcKenziesLand

Also follow Kitty's grandchildren's lives in *Southern Sons*. Also available in Kindle, paperback, large print and audio.
http://myBook.to/SouthernSons

Ms Brear has done it again. She quickly became one on my 'must read' list.
−The Romance Studio

Ms. Brear's character development has certainly impressed me.
Kudos to the author. - Diane Wylie - author

AnneMarie Brear

Australian born, AnneMarie Brear's ancestry is true Yorkshire going back centuries.

Her love of reading fiction started at an early age with Enid Blyton's novels, before moving on into more adult stories such as Catherine Cookson's novels as a teenager.

Living in England, she discovered her love of history by visiting the many and varied places of historical interest.

The road to publication was long and winding with a few false starts, but she finally became published in 2006. Since that time, AnneMarie's has had several novels and short stories published. Her contemporary romance, *Hooked on You,* written under the pen name, Anne Whitfield, was a 2011 finalist for the international EPIC award.

Her books are available in ebook and paperback from bookstores, especially online bookstores. Please feel free to leave a review online if you enjoyed Kitty McKenzie.

For more about AnneMarie Brear and her books visit her website where you can subscribe to her newsletter.
http://www.annemariebrear.com
Facebook:
http://www.facebook.com/annemariebrear

Printed in Great Britain
by Amazon